"Why didn't you kiss me last night?"

"Why should I have?" Daniel said, shooting her a bad-boy grin.

"Because you probably kiss all your female bosses," Jo teased. "But I suppose you're getting sick of it."

"No, I just wasn't sure you'd want me to." He smiled.

"I see," she whispered. She wanted his kiss, his lips on hers and his strong arms around her. She thought it was obvious, but maybe he needed some encouragement.

She moved toward him. Before she knew it, his arms were around her, and she and Daniel were lost in one another. Nothing mattered but his kiss, his arms and the explosive need she felt for him.

Nothing…except for the sound of shattering glass that forced them apart as quickly as if a bomb had just exploded between them….

ABOUT THE AUTHOR

Laura Pender lives in the Minneapolis, Minnesota, region with her two children and her spouse, who contributes heavily to her Harlequin Intrigue novels. A prolific writer, she has written for *Alfred Hitchcock's Mystery Magazine* and many other publications.

Books by Laura Pender

Don't miss any of our special offers. Write to us at the following address for information on our newest releases.

Harlequin Reader Service
U.S.: 3010 Walden Ave., P.O. Box 1325, Buffalo, NY 14269
Canadian: P.O. Box 609, Fort Erie, Ont. L2A 5X3

Midnight Rider

Laura Pender

Harlequin Books

TORONTO • NEW YORK • LONDON
AMSTERDAM • PARIS • SYDNEY • HAMBURG
STOCKHOLM • ATHENS • TOKYO • MILAN
MADRID • WARSAW • BUDAPEST • AUCKLAND

ISBN 0-373-22280-7

MIDNIGHT RIDER

This edition published by arrangement with Harlequin Enterprises B. V.

® and TM are trademarks of the publisher. Trademarks indicated with ® are registered in the United States Patent and Trademark Office, the Canadian Trade Marks Office and in other countries.

Printed in U.S.A.

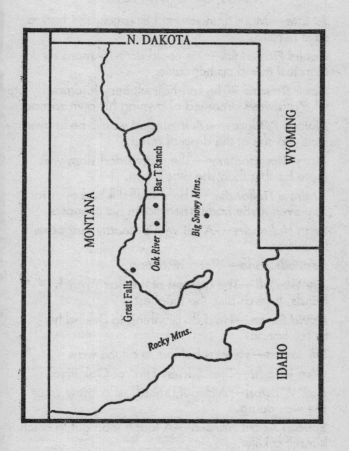

CAST OF CHARACTERS

Jo Tate—More than saving her ranch, she had to save her life.

Daniel Fitzpatrick—He could do a lot more for Jo than just round up her cattle.

Hank Driscoll—The red-haired, fiery foreman who'd always dreamed of owning his own spread.

Norton Pettigrew—A frustrated would-be lawyer, ready to sue at the drop of a hat.

Mary Montgomery—The redheaded siren was more trouble than she was worth.

Andrew Hollander—The sheriff still had eyes for Jo—even if she had turned down his proposal.

Evan Hollander—A vet with a deadly diagnosis to deliver.

Kenneth Zane—Not a nice man.

Jay Westall—The quietest of the Bar T ranch hands, he was also the toughest.

David Burke—He'd do anything to defend his boss's honor.

Bill James—He was behind Jo all the way.

Glen Wright—The "Barney Fife" of Oak River.

Gail Winston—A deputy sheriff who knew what she was doing.

Special Agent Harden—A tough man out to catch himself a killer.

Prologue

It was after midnight when the tanker truck bounced over the rutted old road. The moon was bright overhead, but that didn't make the road any easier to navigate in the dark, and the trucker cursed under his breath as he drove. After what seemed like an eternity, he came upon a Jeep parked near the scar of a gravel pit dug into the prairie. Following the waved directions of a man standing by the Jeep, he drove past the quarry and stopped, backing the end of the long tank just a bit off the road.

"You're late!" The man lit a cigarette and waited for the driver to get down from the cab.

"It's dark, you fool," the trucker countered. "I thought we were making daylight runs on this site."

"The old man's been nosing around." The man drew deeply on his cigarette, exhaled a long plume of smoke and watched it drift through the glare of the Jeep's headlights. "Just get on with it and stop complaining."

"That old man could be trouble." The trucker moved to the back of the tank and opened the outlet valve at its base. A heavy stream of liquid splashed onto the packed earth and ran away in a thickening stream. "This whole setup is pretty lame."

"Mind your own business."

The two men stood silent for a moment watching the liquid gush out of the tank onto the prairie floor. A cow lowed in the darkness nearby, answered by another farther away.

"You should at least move the herd away," the trucker said.

"The old man wants to graze the land. I can't stop him."

"You'll have to sooner or later."

"We're hoping old age will get him first. Of course, we can always arrange for an accident."

"You'd better arrange it. We could do a lot more business up here if he wasn't slowing us down."

"We'll take care of him. Just as soon as everything is set to get the ranch, we can get rid of the old man."

They continued talking as the liquid ran down into a broadening pool before them.

The cattle moved slightly as they drowsed, annoyed by the smell that rose on the light breeze and drifted away to the east.

The wind carried the smell of death, losing its intensity as it traveled, until it was undetectable. But it was still there, floating on the wind to touch lives beyond those of the sleeping cattle.

And the stain of death would remain on the virgin earth for a long time.

Chapter One

Joanne "Jo" Tate stood on the wide porch of her house and looked over the ranch yard with satisfaction. It was her third year as owner of the Bar T Ranch, and it looked as though their profits would be up again this year. Not a bad record for a ranch in a recession and facing a public that had lost much of its taste for red meat. Not bad at all. She was proud of her accomplishments as a rancher and felt that her father would not be disappointed, if he could see her now.

Her father, Jonas Tate, had expressed great faith in her ability to run the ranch. And to make certain that his faith was well founded, he had worked her as hard as any of the hired hands when she was a teenager. She worked the ranch until she knew every phase of the operation and could single-handedly deal with any task that came up. Then, after years of treating her more like a son than a daughter, Jonas Tate had sent his daughter off to college to get the "rough edges sanded off" and to let her know something about her options in the world. He was a worldly man who had served in the state senate for two terms and had traveled extensively, so he wanted his daughter to know something of the larger world, as well.

Jo knew that if she'd decided against returning to ranching, he would have supported her decision gladly, for personal freedom had always been a prime tenet of his philosophy. But he'd clearly been proud and gratified that she'd decided to come back home to Montana after getting her business degree. While Jonas Tate had probably been unsure about her plans for her future, Joanne Tate had no doubt at all. She loved the land and had never considered any other course but to return to the land that had nurtured her all her life.

Now, three years after her father's untimely death, the twenty-nine-year-old rancher couldn't help but feel pride swell within her at what she'd accomplished as the head of the Bar T. She felt that she had done her father's memory proud and vowed to ensure that the ranch remain intact and viable for future generations of Tates. No matter what direction she might turn her clear blue eyes, it was all Tate land, and that is what it would remain.

Of course, the next generation wouldn't be Tates, would they? Well, they would be if she had anything to say about it. Joanne Tate wasn't about to give up her name for anyone and was determined to keep the Tate name over the iron gate of her ranch.

She smiled in wonder at how her mind had moved quickly from thoughts of the coming roundup, to her father, then on to future generations. But for there to be future generations of any name, there had to be a mister in the present, and as her friend Mary Montgomery was fond of saying, "pickings are slim in these parts." Not that there hadn't been offers, just that they never came from the right man.

The whole thing troubled her, too. Like her father, Jo put great stock in the family and their continuing stewardship of the land. She wasn't about to let the fourth generation of Tates be the last to run the Bar T Ranch— but she wasn't about to settle for less than what she wanted. Mary had done just that, and she'd ended up divorced and lonely not long after her marriage to the quarterback of the high school football team. And from what Jo had seen of her friend's current beau, Mary was still settling.

At the moment, however, Jo wasn't looking for a husband but a helicopter pilot to help with the cattle. He was overdue at the ranch, and she'd been absently watching the road for any sign of an approaching car. It wasn't a good sign if the man was late his first day, but since he was new to the area, she would give him the benefit of the doubt.

In the tight economics of ranching, manpower was often the most expensive part of the operation, and, with over seven thousand acres, it took a fair number of ranch hands to keep the cattle on the Bar T Ranch in line. The modern addition of all-terrain vehicles and moderate use of fencing helped, of course, but they still needed at least six hands to tend the cattle and the eight hundred acres of wheat, which she'd started last year to expand the operation a bit. And the coming roundup presented a special problem in controlling the herd—six was a small number, but the four hands who were actually available made it almost impossible.

It was her foreman, Hank Driscoll's idea that they might do without the two extra men if they had a good man with a helicopter overhead. He had pressed the issue with his reluctant boss, citing countless cases of ranchers benefiting from aerial help, until he had won her over—to a point.

Looking at the balance sheet and estimating the cost of aviation fuel along with a man's salary, Jo had conceded the possibility of a savings, but she wasn't certain that she wanted to put up with the noise. The countryside was too peaceful to be intruded upon, and helicopters were notoriously noisy.

It was so peaceful here, too.

On a morning like this, Jo could imagine just how peaceful it had been when the Tates first came to Montana territory. The breeze made a sibilant hiss in the trees, their branches shivering, then lying still. Birds flitted about amid the leaves, calling out to one another. And beyond the yard, the grass moved in wavelike ripples as the wind swept over the land, this big beautiful land of hers.

Yes, the quiet was exquisite, she thought as she slipped her fingers through her long, blond hair and leaned against the porch rail, drinking in the cool, lightly scented air. She could very easily imagine the vast country as it had been over a hundred years ago; it was still a large, peaceful country. It was still, in many ways, the last frontier.

But the stillness of the countryside began to change slowly, gaining a low throbbing hum that grew quickly and increased in volume behind the ranch house. Suddenly, the noise burst overhead like an explosion, as the shadow of a helicopter passed over her and on into the yard between the bunkhouse and corral. The craft swung around and hovered like a dragon looking for victims on the ground.

Jo squinted up at the aircraft as it lowered itself, scattering the birds and sending swirling clouds of dust up into the once-pristine sky. Then the slim-nosed beast settled itself in the yard, and the hellish noise stopped, replaced by the sound of the rotors spinning, a high *whooshing* sound that deepened as they slowed, then finally stopped.

The silence that came after the arrival of the helicopter was more absolute than the silence that had preceded it. There were no birds chirping now, and even the wind had stopped, as if in awe of the sheer concentration of force the aircraft had brought along with it. Jo stood watching the gleaming white beast, somewhat in awe, herself, that anything could be as quiet as the world seemed at that moment. The only time it was ever this quiet was just before a storm.

Then the birds found their voices again, and the spell was broken. Jo stepped off the porch and walked toward the helicopter, not sure she was interested in hiring a man whose mode of transportation was so noisy.

One side of the Plexiglas canopy lifted as she approached it, and a man unfolded himself from one of the two seats and stepped down. A tall, sandy-haired fellow, the pilot grinned broadly as they met in the yard. "Is this the Tate place?" he drawled as he extended his hand. His eyes were hidden behind a pair of aviator glasses, but the smile below them was friendly and guileless. "Jo Tate?"

"Yes," Jo said. For a brief moment, she had been tempted to deny possession of the name and send him off to become someone else's problem, but sanity prevailed. "You're Mr. Fitzpatrick?"

"Daniel, please." His grip was firm and sure as he shook her hand, two efficient pumps. "The way I fly, I may not live long enough to get on a first-name basis if I don't get there fast." He removed his protective glasses, revealing a pair of lively green eyes that sparkled in the hot sun and seemed to bore through to the young ranch owner's soul.

Jo laughed. She liked straightforward men, and though he might be a bit glib for her taste, he was definitely straightforward.

"In that case, call me Jo." She walked past him and slipped her hands into the front pockets of her jeans as she studied the helicopter closely. "So this is the future of ranching," she said. "Makes a lot of racket, doesn't it?"

"I suppose it does," he admitted. "And I don't know about the future of ranching, but I've done all right with it. I would have thought with a spread this size, you would have been using a chopper for years now."

"No, we made do with extra men. You have worked a ranch before, haven't you?"

"Yes, though I haven't done much of it," he said honestly. "My uncle owns a ranch in Texas, and I helped him with it a bit after I got out of the service."

"Good. My foreman thinks you can save us some money and he's never been far wrong before. Were the figures you gave him accurate or were they just a ploy to get hired?"

"They are accurate." Daniel patted the side of his ship, leaving a handprint in the dust that had settled over it. "I stripped this baby down when I bought it. Got the excess weight out. I get pretty good mileage, and I try not to price myself out of business. Depends on your wages, but I figure I cost about a man and a half at most."

"About that." She nodded.

"Of course, I'm not looking to replace anyone. Did you lose some help or are you planning some layoffs?" He leaned against the helicopter, squinting at her as though he were conducting the interview and she wasn't doing very well.

"Two of my men quit over the last month. They moved on. A third one may be getting a spread of his own, so I might be down by three soon." She didn't really expect Hank to find a ranch, but he had been talking about it. That was one of the reasons he had suggested hiring a pilot, so he could move on with a clear conscience.

"That's all right, then." He smiled, his straight white teeth catching the sunlight and seeming to gleam in his tanned face. "So, what else do you need to know about me? You've got my résumé."

"Yes, and it looks very good. Four years as an army pilot? Were you in the Gulf War?"

"Yes, I was in that show—what there was of it." He patted the helicopter again, smoothing its sleek skin as Jo might smooth the shoulder of her horse after a ride. "She's a beauty for cattle."

"I don't recognize the model. Not that I should, I suppose, but it looks different from most helicopters I've seen." It was a long, narrow machine with a low, pointed snout, a pair of stubby wings about midway along the fuselage and a long tail stretching wasp-like behind it. The rotors hung overhead like long swords waiting to slice through the air. "Seems bigger than most," she added.

"You don't see these in commercial use. This ship is a Bell AH-1G Huey Cobra attack helicopter," he said proudly. "Army surplus. It's been stripped of weaponry and most of the high-tech doodads, but it still handles like a dream and turns so fast you could get dizzy watching it."

"Is it legal to own military aircraft?" It was odd to think of anyone herding cattle using a machine designed for warfare—it was like picturing a crop duster plying his trade in an F-16.

"If you go to the right auctions, it is. They don't like to take chances on metal fatigue if they're going into battle. In fact, they upgrade their aircraft more often than the airlines do."

"But you still fly it?"

"She's airworthy," he insisted. "You've got some crop flyers going around in sixty-three-year-old biplanes. My Cobra's only got twenty years on her, and they haven't found a better design yet. The Cobra is still the army's standard gunship."

"Fine, just don't call it a gunship. I'm only just getting used to the idea of having a helicopter on the place—a gunship is too much to take."

"Got it. Want to go up for a spin?"

"I don't think that's necessary," Jo told him. "I'll just take your word for its condition."

"Come on, you'll love it. See the place from a whole new perspective. You sit up front where the gunnery officer used to sit, so you can see forever. And there's lots of room with the weapons system out."

To illustrate his point, he popped open the hinged canopy and pulled himself up on the steel rail of the landing gear to look inside. Jo joined him more out of courtesy than curiosity, looking in at the cockpit, which held two seats, one in back of the other. There was a surprising amount of room inside, though most of it was taken up by a set of canvas suitcases in the nose of the ship.

"The front seat was for the weapons officer," Daniel explained. "He ran the machine gun and cannons, while the jockey steered behind him. Plenty of legroom now.''

''Well, I think I'll pass on your offer at the moment, but we'll plan on a trip real soon.''

She'd have to go up sometime, of course, but she wanted to see how well he flew before risking her life with the man. She didn't care for flying, and all she'd ever heard about helicopter pilots was that they were wild and somewhat irrational. Though he didn't seem irrational, she could see a wild streak in his pride concerning the aircraft. If given the chance, she was afraid he'd put her through an ordeal somewhat like being strapped into a roller coaster without brakes.

''Anytime.'' He stepped down, dusting his hands off on his jeans. ''So, am I hired?''

''Yes, Mr. Fitzpatrick, I'll give you a chance.''

''Great. And remember, my name is Daniel. Dan is even better.'' Then he laughed, adding, ''And I was exaggerating earlier. I don't really fly that dangerously. Haven't killed anyone yet.''

''I'm sure you haven't. Come up to the house and fill out some insurance forms. Then I'll show you to your room.''

''Nice place,'' he commented as they walked together to the two-story house standing amid cottonwood and oak trees. ''How many head do you run here?''

''Up to a hundred thousand or so. We've got about as many as we can feed right now, and in dry years we run about fifteen percent less.'' She spoke about her operation with great pride, noting the similarity between the way he spoke of his helicopter and the way she spoke about the ranch. Maybe they had more in common than she thought.

They entered the house, its dark interior welcome after the glare of the sun nearing its zenith. A comfortable house without ostentation, the Tate home was decorated in earth tones that welcomed visitors with a homey feeling that was quite natural, rather than imposed by some decorator. Clean and tidy, the house, nevertheless, had a lived-in feeling, the sense that people actually carried on their daily lives within its walls and that those people weren't the type to put on airs. In other words, it didn't look like a millionaire's home, though on paper, Jo Tate certainly was that.

She walked through the living room to the office, where she sat in an oak swivel chair behind a massive rolltop desk. She extracted a form from one of the cubbyholes and handed it and a pen to her new employee.

"This will make you a member of our group insurance policy," she told him as she stood. "Heaven knows what a helicopter pilot will do to our rates, but I don't suppose that can be helped."

"Blow them through the roof, probably," he said, laughing. "I haven't had insurance for years."

"Pull up a chair. Would you like a glass of lemonade?"

"I'd love one, boss." He sat at the desk, looking over the insurance form.

"Can you cook?" she asked from the doorway.

"In a pinch, sure."

"Good. We usually rotate cooking around here. It makes for variety and lets the guys get out of the sun from time to time. Of course, if you can't cook, we'll excuse you from kitchen duty."

"Wait till you taste my meat loaf," he boasted. "And do you like lasagna?"

"We'll see."

Jo walked to the kitchen feeling better about him. His aircraft may be noisy, but at least he wasn't. While there was something of the swaggering daredevil about him, he wasn't the wild man straight out of a low-budget war picture that she'd expected. And the glibness she'd detected at first seemed to be more a friendly openness than any kind of salesman's banter.

Daniel Fitzpatrick would fit in well on the ranch. She could see that much already. The man intrigued her personally, too, though she couldn't quite put her finger on what it was about him that she liked.

She opened the refrigerator in the brightly modern kitchen and took out the pitcher of lemonade. Taking two glasses down from the cupboard, she was just filling them when the front door opened, and the heavy tread of boots on the hardwood floor sounded through the house.

"Jo! You here, Jo?" It was Hank Driscoll calling her name urgently.

"In the kitchen, Hank!" She put the pitcher down, something in the severe tone of his voice alerting her that she might not have time for a beverage at the moment. "What's up?" she asked when the stocky redhead came in holding his Stetson in one hand and rubbing his bandanna across his damp forehead with the other.

"We've got some dead cattle," he said quickly. "Ten of them in the north range."

"Dead? Ten of them? How?"

"It looks like they got into something. Whatever it was, looks to have hit them all at the same time. Probably overnight."

"We'd better have a look at them." She put the lemonade back into the fridge and took her own hat from the peg on the wall. "Let's go."

"Good, you can have your ride now," Dan said from the doorway. "I can have you on the site in no time."

"No, I'd rather—"

But Hank cut her off, saying, "Good idea, Jo. You might as well try the new guy out right off." Hank turned toward Dan, thrusting his hand toward him. "I see you made it," he said. "I'm Hank Driscoll. We spoke on the telephone."

"Dan Fitzpatrick. Glad to meet you. The directions you sent me were on the money." He took Hank's hand, shaking it with the same efficient double pump as he had with Jo. "These cattle, are they due north?"

"Northwest as the crow flies," Hank said, adding for Jo's benefit, "about twenty miles, in a gully just off the west service road."

"All right, then," she said, frowning. "Hank, call Doc Hollander. Well . . . I guess I'm going flying."

ONCE SHE WAS STRAPPED into the seat ahead of his with the helmet on her head, Jo felt as though she'd been swallowed by some mechanical monster. In her estimation, this was no way to herd cattle and certainly no way for civilized human beings to travel around.

Dan flipped some switches behind her, and the engine started up with a rising whine—except that this time she was within the roar of the beast. The noise and vibration seemed to make her heart stop for a moment, and she couldn't help but remember the sick feeling she always got as a child just before the roller coaster started up the first incline.

"Here we go!" Dan's voice crackled over the headset in the helmet, which hung loosely on her head, and before she could move the microphone on her helmet around to reply, they were, indeed, on their way.

They didn't rise so much as leap into the air. Jo's stomach plummeted and she gripped the handles on either side of her with white-knuckled force as the ranch buildings suddenly dropped out of sight, seemingly swallowed up by the ground. Then the buildings were in view again as Dan put the chopper into motion, tilting to the right as he swung the craft around and hurried north before they were even above the treetops. The branches of the oak near the corral swept by all too close to the Plexiglas canopy that suddenly seemed way too thin as they skimmed only about a foot over the roof of the bunkhouse.

Suddenly, the obstructions were gone, and all she could see from her sunken position was blue sky. The helicopter flew so smoothly, it didn't even feel as if they were flying. When she sat up and looked out, their flight was readily apparent, though. The rolling hills rushed below them, the wind from the rotor blades pressing a moving circle of flattened vegetation like a shadow in the grass.

Seeing their motion, she wished she hadn't looked, because they couldn't have been more than ten feet above the ground, and they were following the terrain as precisely as if they were running on a track below.

"Keep a lookout for your cattle," he said, his voice crackling in her ears.

"Can't you fly higher?" Jo was surprised that she had any voice at all.

"Going up wastes time. Besides, if something goes wrong, I won't have to fall too far." He laughed, loudly, in her helmet. "Okay, we'll take her up."

The helicopter tilted on its tail, straight up, then levelling off several hundred feet above the ground. It seemed to Jo that it took a full minute for her stomach to catch up with them.

"This better?"

"Yes," she said feebly as she fought to keep her stomach in place. "Remind me never to do this again."

"Hey, now, I've never crashed one of these things yet! There's a road down there. Should I follow that?"

"Yes." She leaned to look down, spotting the ranch service road. "Follow it north. It's about three miles to the gully."

"Right, boss."

He slipped them into a turn, giving her the feeling that her bottom was sliding out from under her while her head remained in place. Then they shot ahead again, pressing her back into her seat.

Seconds later the gully was in view, with dark shapes apparent on the slope to the small water hole at its base.

"You'd better land upwind of them," she shouted into her mouthpiece.

And almost as soon as she'd said the word, they were down, landing lightly in the tall, summer-browned grass at the top of the slope. The roar cut off, leaving them in silence until he popped open the canopy of the craft and the sound of the revolving rotors could be heard. When the rotors stopped, he got out and helped her from her seat.

Jo would gladly have kissed the ground once she was on it, but she wasn't about to give him the satisfaction of knowing how much his aerobatics had affected her. She had been all too right about the roller coaster.

"Do you always fly like that?"

"Whenever I get the chance." He was laughing. "That's the way I was taught to fly."

"What kind of sadist taught you that?"

"The army."

"Not a good way to start a new job, is it? Making your boss sick, I mean?"

"Sure it is. *Especially* with a new employer. I want you to know firsthand that I know what I'm doing. This wasn't much of a ride, though. I can do better."

"You did well enough."

"You do look awfully white, Jo. But you did better than a lot of people. Most of them throw up once they get back on the ground."

"Oh," she said, laughing lamely, "I'm so proud of myself."

But he was right about one thing; she was now quite certain he was a good pilot. She was also certain he was nuts. But that was probably a requirement of his occupation.

Turning to the matter at hand, Jo walked down the hill toward the dead cattle. When she got to the first carcass, she stopped, frowning down it.

"Oh, this is just wonderful," she said. "Didn't that fool Hank even look at them?"

"What?" Dan came up beside her, his eyes hidden behind his sunglasses as he regarded her.

"Dead animals are bad enough, but these aren't our cattle."

"Somebody grazing on your land?"

"Probably. They belong to Norton Pettigrew, and he's certainly not above using our land if he thinks he can get away with it. Of course, he'll say they strayed and then try to make me pay for their death," she said. "This just isn't good at all."

"Maybe they were diseased. Could infect your herd."

"It doesn't look that way," she said. "The vet will be out soon, and he should be able to tell us. I just hope it wasn't anything they picked up here. I don't need trouble with Pettigrew."

"Is he that bad?"

"If there's a chance at a profit he is," she said thoughtfully. "But I'll be darned if I'm going to give him satisfaction for anything that happened to cattle on my land illegally."

"Sounds like a range war," Dan said drolly.

"Once you meet Pettigrew, you won't think that's very funny," Jo said.

At this point, she thought, the modern equivalent of a range war was all too possible.

Chapter Two

Evan Hollander, the veterinarian who had served the ranchers around Oak River, Montana, for thirty years, stood over the dead cattle and ran his gnarled fingers through the unruly thatch of gray hair that stuck out beneath the bill of his baseball cap. He frowned, walking around the dead animals and examining them once more. Then he cleared his throat, spat into the dry grass on the side of the hill and shrugged his shoulders as he looked over the horizon.

"Don't look like they were ill," he said at last. "Something they ate, most likely, though I'll be damned if I can say what would kill them all at once like that. Have to run a bunch of tests on one of the carcasses."

"Can you make a guess right now?" Jo asked. She stood beside the vet, her hands in the front pockets of her jeans as she shifted restlessly from one foot to the other. "I won't hold you to it, but I'd sure like to have an idea of some kind."

"No, I can't guess," he answered. "Too damn many things can kill cattle. Saw three cows dead on a spread north of here, all swelled up, and we couldn't figure what killed them. Turned out to be snakebites of all the damn things. I would've never guessed that in dog's years, but there it was.''

"Snakes?'' Dan shuffled his feet, eyeing the tall grass suspiciously. "Could a snake kill a big animal like this?''

"The cows stepped into a nest of them,'' the old vet replied. "Got bit many times. 'Course, they swelled from the venom, so we couldn't see the bites.''

"What do we do now?'' Jo asked.

"I'll have to haul one of them in for an autopsy. You can let the animal-disposal boys take the rest as soon as we know what killed them.''

"How long will it take to figure out the cause of death?''

"Depends on a bunch of things,'' he said, considering the question. "Maybe I'll find it's something easy. Then it's a day maybe. If not, I'll have to send blood samples to a lab for tests.''

"I'll get some hands up here to help load the body into your truck,'' Jo said.

"I can load it,'' Dan offered. "I've got a couple of long ropes in the chopper. That would speed things up a bit, wouldn't it?''

"With your helicopter?'' The older man eyed the craft speculatively. "I wouldn't think that thing was capable of so subtle a maneuver.''

"We can be subtle when we want to be,'' Dan said, grinning as he walked over to his helicopter on the crest of the hill. "Usually, there's just not much cause for it.''

"That's an army job, isn't it?'' Doc Hollander took off his cap and swabbed his forehead with a handkerchief. "Looks like one of those attack choppers they had all over TV a while back.''

"Yes, sir," Dan replied. He took two stout nylon ropes from inside the cockpit and knelt down to tie them onto the vertical supports for the landing skids. "Huey Cobra."

"Yeah, thought so. I worked a M.A.S.H. unit in Korea and flew a lot of boys out on that monster's ancestor. Looks kinda puny next to that one," he said, putting his cap back on.

"Yes, sir, she's a fine craft," Dan said, standing once more. "Okay, I'll come down overhead, and you can tie the ropes on so I can lift it. Just give me the sign when I'm low enough, and then again when you're ready for me to lift."

"Don't fall on us," Jo warned.

"Oh, I probably won't," Dan said as he climbed into the cockpit and brought the machine to life. "But, you're insured, aren't you?"

Jo and Doc Hollander clung to their hats, as the flying machine created a hurricane in the once-still air, and watched as it rose and slipped across to hover over the animals, the two ropes dangling below it. In a moment, they had secured the ropes and then stood back as he lifted the carcass and lowered it gently into the box of the veterinarian's battered pickup.

"These are Pettigrew cattle, aren't they?" Doc Hollander commented as the helicopter moved away to land a moment later. "Have you called old Norton yet?"

"No," Jo said levelly. "Haven't been to a phone yet."

"No matter what killed them, you can't dispose of the cattle until you notify the owner."

"I know, and that's why I was hoping you could tell me right away what killed them. He'll raise a stink." Jo spoke sourly as she watched Dan step out of the chopper. "I'd sure like to know it wasn't anything on my property that killed them."

"Well, I can't help you there," the vet told her thoughtfully. "Not yet, anyway. But they were twenty miles off his land. He ought to keep better track of his animals."

"You know Norton. He's not going to care about a little thing like that."

"Ready to fly?" Dan asked as he joined them.

"No," she answered. "But I don't reckon that I want to walk."

"I'll do the best I can to hurry this up," Doc Hollander told her. "Maybe I can get Andy to put a priority rush on the blood sample," he added, referring to his nephew, Andrew Hollander, the county sheriff. "It was nice meeting you, son," he said to Dan as he shook his hand. "Maybe I can cage a ride in that thing some day."

"Anytime, Doc."

"Thanks, Evan," Jo said to the older man. "I'll be in touch real soon." She stood watching for a moment as the veterinarian got into his pickup. Then, she turned to Dan. "Let's get this over with. I've got to call Norton Pettigrew."

"You want to just fly over and tell him in person?"

"Hell, no," she said, laughing. "He'd sue us for upsetting his laying hens. Besides, the last thing I want to do is talk to Norton Pettigrew in person."

"I DON'T KNOW what killed them," she was telling the other rancher ten minutes later. A tall glass of lemonade was waiting on the counter, frosty and inviting, as a reward for making the call, and she sat at her kitchen table watching water bead up on the sides of the glass, while listening to Norton Pettigrew rant on the other end of the line.

"If you poisoned my cattle, Jo Tate, I'll expect double damages on the beef," he said. "You people can't just kill off my herd, bury the evidence, and expect to get away with it."

"We haven't buried anything," she told him. "You can come and do that yourself if you wish. I sure won't stop you. Besides, you know that Evan Hollander isn't going to cover up the results."

"I don't know anything of the kind."

"Oh, Norton, I'm awful sorry about your cattle, and I promise to make good if it was my fault," she said, fighting to maintain a calm voice, despite the seething need to shout the man down, "but you did kind of let them wander a bit, didn't you? I should be charging you for grazing if that's the way you run your ranch."

"I run my ranch the way I want to run it, and I won't have a pup telling me how. We run open range up here, Jo, so don't start trying to bully me."

"I'm not bullying anyone, but your open range is only in your mind. I'm just telling you what happened. You can call Evan yourself for the results."

"Don't think I won't do that, Tate," the rancher insisted. "Don't think for a moment that I won't."

"Goodbye, Norton," Jo said, skewing her expressive lips into a sour scowl. "Take care now." She hung up before he had a chance to reply.

"I take it he's not exactly a friendly neighbor." Dan stepped through the kitchen door with his hat in his hand and stood smiling at Jo.

"Do you always listen in on conversations?" she asked abruptly, scowling at him.

"Only if it's not too much work," he said casually. He pulled a chair back from the table and lowered his lanky form onto it, then removed his sunglasses and placed them on the table. "And you weren't exactly quiet, you know."

"I'm sorry," she said. "I didn't mean to snap at you just now. It's just that—"

"That your neighbor is a jerk but you don't want to upset him," he completed. "It's hard to be nice when you'd like nothing better than to club him over the head with something."

Dan stood and walked over to take her glass of lemonade from the counter and bring it to her. "You probably need this."

"I'll probably need more than that before I'm through with this business," she said. "But thank you very much."

"Anytime, boss." He sat across from her and watched her drink her lemonade, a strange smile spreading across his lips. He didn't say anything, but, after a moment, he settled back into his chair with a sigh and folded his arms across his chest, his wonderful green eyes holding her in their gaze. "So, what kind of trouble do you expect from this guy?"

"I'll handle it, don't worry." Jo put her glass down, returning his gaze in kind. "I've dealt with Pettigrew before, you know."

She found that she enjoyed looking at him. An aura of confidence surrounded him, seeming to add to the luster of his eyes and the openness of his smile. Oddly enough, just looking at him made her feel good.

"I'm not worried," he said after a moment. "I never worry, if I can help it. But it sounds like you've had trouble with this guy before. If I'm working here, it'll be my trouble, too. I just want to be prepared.''

"Aside from the fact that he's an ornery cuss, I don't have any problems with the man. He's a walking lawsuit," she explained. "If he paid as much attention to his ranch as he does to potential excuses to drag neighbors into court, he'd be a lot better off.''

"Not much of a rancher, is he?" Dan asked.

"Better than he used to be," Jo said. "He nearly ran the spread into the ground a few years back, but he's managed to get it back in shape since then. He seems to be all right now." Then she laughed, allowing herself to relax a bit and sit with one arm casually looped over the back of the chair. "I think he's really just a frustrated lawyer," she said. "That's why he spends all of his free time suing people.''

"Where I come from, we string up lawyers," Dan said affably.

"Oh, really? That was Texas, you said?"

"Texas, originally. I've been around some since then.''

"Yes, I suppose they do hang lawyers down there.''

"But we only hang them when we're feeling feisty," he told her. "Usually, we just shoot them.''

"Don't they wear boots in Texas?" she commented, nodding toward the running shoe that graced the foot he had casually crossed over one knee.

"Sure." He nodded. "I never liked boots, though. They hurt my toes.''

"Great, a cowboy with sensitive feet.''

"I'm no cowboy, I'm a pilot," he replied easily.

"Well, you might want to invest in a pair of square-toed boots, then. Ranching is too rough and dusty for tennis shoes.''

"Flying chopper isn't the least bit dusty."

"We might need your help in other areas, though," she told him. "You'll be sorry."

"I'd be a lot sorrier if I had to break in a new pair of boots." He laughed, stretching back in his chair. "By the way, I don't ride, either."

"What?" Jo grinned and took a refreshing sip of her drink. "Don't tell the other men, or they'll be no end of trouble for you."

"I imagine they'll find out soon enough." He smiled, still regarding her with quiet amusement.

"I can't believe that you're a Texas boy and you don't ride a horse."

"I'm a city Texan," he explained. "My old man was in stocks and bonds, oil, gas, whatever was going on at the time. My uncle ran the ranch. The rest of the family are politicians. I probably know more about stock options and greenmail than I do about ranching."

"Oh, great, I've gone and hired the only Texan in the world who can't ride and who doesn't know ranching. What did you do with your youth? Junior arbitrage?"

"Oh, the usual. We drove around in pickup trucks and shot highway signs with pistols. You know, Texas kid stuff."

"Now you're pulling my leg."

"Well, now, I don't suppose I did anything much different than any other wayward youth. I just didn't do much of it on horseback."

"How did you get into flying? Was it part of your army training?"

"No, I flew small planes in high school and college. I didn't get the bug for choppers until a friend of mine took me up. She did her best to make me sick up there, too."

"Oh, that's a tradition with you people, is it?" Jo smiled, enjoying the conversation as it turned away from her current problems. He was easy to talk to and easier still to listen to.

"We'd lose our self-esteem if anyone left their first ride smiling." He laughed. "Don't ever accept a ride in an F-14 if you thought my flying was bad. The greatest thrill a jet jockey has is making passengers blow lunch."

"So, this friend of yours turned you on to helicopters? Why go into the army?"

"My father paid for my flying lessons, but by that time I was on my own. I couldn't afford the air time. I figured I could stand four years in the army."

"You probably didn't count on having a war while you were in, did you?"

"No, ma'am, but that was okay. Not much to it, really. So what about this neighbor?" he said, changing the subject. "How much trouble do you expect from him?"

"He's got so many lawyers, I reckon it'll be easier to just pay for the cattle," she said. "But I sure won't if I don't have to. I don't like him running his cattle at will on my range. Open range, my butt," she snarled. "I'll open-range him if I catch any more of his diseased animals on my land."

"So do you think we're in for a fight?" Dan said eagerly.

"Everything is a fight with Pettigrew."

"I'll keep my eyes open," he said. "I don't mind a fight, but I sure don't want to go into it blindly."

"I'm talking about a *legal* battle, Daniel, not a shoot-out at high noon."

"I know." But he laughed.

"It didn't sound like you knew it."

He smiled, standing once more. "I don't know what kind of run-ins you've had with this jasper in the past, but once two ranchers start arguing about cattle, all hell usually breaks loose."

Jo finished her lemonade and stood with him, smiling. "This is the nineties, Daniel," she reminded him.

"So you say." Dan put his sunglasses on, hiding the eyes above his broad smile behind their reflective surface. "So you say. I'll go unpack my stuff."

"You do that," she said. "Maybe you'd like to come into town with us tonight and take a look around. No sense in being shy, and I sure want to blow off some steam after today."

"You're the boss," Dan said as he walked out of the kitchen.

What ever the pilot might think, Jo didn't envision things going that far over a few head of cattle. Not even with Pettigrew. As she watched the new man walk through the living room and out the front door of her comfortable house, Jo wondered exactly what he thought he was getting into and why he seemed to look forward to a conflict. That didn't make any sense to her at all.

But then, men in general didn't make sense to Jo. They could work like mules and were loyal to a fault, traits she appreciated and admired, but it seemed that fighting and wagering were what they loved best. Maybe that was the type of man it took to work a ranch, or maybe that was just the type of man who was attracted to the solitude and open spaces of ranching. Was Daniel Fitzpatrick cut from that same cloth?

She found herself hoping that he wasn't. He seemed to have a good head on his shoulders and he kept it cool, too. He didn't seem the kind to go off half-cocked and get himself into trouble the way many of the hands had done in the past. After all, he'd been in combat, where a hotheaded nature wouldn't do.

Still, there was something about him that seemed to indicate there was more to him than met the eye. Something she couldn't quite put her finger on told her to keep an eye on that one. Oh, yes, she would definitely keep her eye on him.

Jo walked to her room, wondering if this horseless Texan at least knew how to dance.

DAN HAULED his two duffel bags into the bunkhouse and found an empty bed in one of the rooms. The house had four rooms: a main room, which served as a kitchen, dining room and living room in one, a bathroom, and two bedrooms with four beds in each. Contrary to the name of his new lodgings, they weren't bunk beds but single beds, each with its own dresser. It wasn't much for privacy, but it was carpeted and it was clean. He couldn't ask for much more than that.

This could be a good thing for him, and he could envision himself staying on here a while. Since he left the army, he had tried a couple areas of commercial aviation without finding his niche. He'd flown helicopter for radio traffic reports in Dallas for a month and then spent a year flying for an eastern corporation, but neither job suited him. They were too confining, and it no longer suited his temperament to spend so much time in the city. It hadn't been until he bought his own helicopter and went west that he began to feel right. But, even there, he was dissatisfied. For, though he'd found the wide-open spaces he had longed for, he had discovered that he couldn't abide them alone.

Maybe as a member of a regular crew, he would feel a part of something. He wasn't good at making friends, but this time he was definitely going to try.

As he unpacked his things, he considered what he may have gotten into here. The surroundings were comfortable, and the job was exactly what he wanted. The pay was all right, and the food promised to be interesting at least. But he might have trouble with his boss, he thought.

Not that she wasn't easy to get along with. She seemed to be a nearly ideal employer so far. No, the problem with her was that she was just too good-looking, and he wasn't sure if he could stand working for someone he might begin to desire.

But, if he were totally honest with himself, he'd have to admit that it wasn't a question of whether or not he "might" desire her. No, as soon as he landed and saw her walking across the yard toward him, he'd felt an unfamiliar tugging inside. The way her dark blond hair reflected the sun had caught his eye and lingered in his mind. She was really too beautiful to work for, since it was never a good policy to ask your boss out on a date.

But, if he didn't ask her out, he might just go crazy. Of course, in a manner of speaking, his boss had already asked him out.

Dan stripped off his shirt, took a fresh one out of the drawer, and laid it on his bed. Then he went across to the bathroom and rinsed the dust away, studying his jaw in the mirror. He should shave, he thought, and then smiled. If he were working for any other rancher, he wouldn't give shaving a thought. It was going to be very awkward working for Jo Tate, but he would just have to endure it.

Stepping back from the mirror, he hitched his jeans up a bit and regarded himself wryly. *Not much there,* he thought. *I'm getting out of shape.* He was a slim, well-muscled man, but the ragged white line of a scar, beginning just below his right breast and wrapping around to the small of his back, broke his even tan. It was an ugly, jagged line of white tissue that resisted the smooth movement of his muscles.

He had suffered the accident that caused the scar when he was fourteen-years old. It was a freak accident. The horse he was riding was frightened by fireworks and bolted through Dan's uncle's front window. The horse had to be put down after the incident, and Dan had spent three months recovering in the hospital. He hadn't ridden a horse since.

His father had suggested cosmetic surgery to cover the scar, but he'd been against it at the time. Now, however, he wished he hadn't been so stubborn. It was ugly, and he felt nasty-looking and flawed every time he looked at it. At the time, he'd been in the hospital too long and was tired of doctors, so he'd decided to live with the scar. He never considered that it would be a constant reminder of the day he gave up riding.

"Hello?" Jo called out from the other room.

"Out in a second." Dan grimaced wryly. If he had only brought a shirt in with him, he wouldn't have to be seen like this. He stepped out of the bathroom. "I'll just get my shirt."

"Oh, I didn't mean to disturb you," she said. Then she stepped toward him, staring. "What in the world happened to you?"

"What?" He stopped turning away from the bedroom door to face her.

"That scar. How did that happen?"

"Oh, well, I had a little accident when I was a kid," he told her, continuing to get his shirt. "Fell through a window." He hoped she wouldn't ask for a more elaborate explanation, because it seemed rather unmanly to him that he'd never returned to riding.

"Oh, that sounds horrible. I can't even stand to imagine that." Jo cringed, images of broken glass and blood flooding her mind unpleasantly.

"It looks worse than it was," he said. He buttoned his shirt quickly.

"It must have been terribly painful," she said. "It doesn't hurt now, does it?"

"Only hurts when I smile," he said, grinning.

"How did you manage to—"

A beeping sound cut her off, and she turned quickly and grabbed the microphone of a radio on the wall by the door.

"Jo here," she said. "Over."

"It's Hank." The foreman's voice was broken by static. "We've got more dead cattle along that draw. They're ours this time. Over."

"How many?" Jo asked urgently.

"Three. Just north of the last site, closer to Pettigrew's spread. Looks the same as the others. Over."

"I'm on my way. Out."

Jo turned back to Dan, frowning. At this point, she wasn't sure which she regretted more, dead cattle or another ride in his helicopter. But it was the fastest way out there, and he was on the payroll.

"I'll bet you want another ride, don't you?" He was grinning, clearly enjoying her discomfort.

"No, I do not," she said. "But I'm stuck with it, aren't I?"

"That's what I'm here for."

"Okay, come on." Jo stepped out of the building and led the way out to the monster waiting in the yard. "But there's no sense trying to make me sick, Daniel. I'm telling you right now that it won't work, so don't bother."

"That sounds like a challenge," he said as he caught up with her and matched her purposeful stride. "Never challenge a Texan, 'cause you may never challenge again."

"Nothing good ever came out of Texas yet," she said, sharply. "And it looks like you're determined to prove that, aren't you?"

"Quite the contrary, boss, I intend to prove that Texans are indispensable."

Chapter Three

"I think that takes care of the stragglers, boss."

Dan's crisp reply to her call on the radio crackled out of the radio receiver hanging from the saddle of Jo's horse. She watched the herd moving slowly along the crest of a low hill toward the east. They had spent the week moving cattle away from Pettigrew land and still weren't finished to her satisfaction. There were over a thousand head on her northwest range that she wanted to move down before the roundup.

Still, she had to admit that the job had been much easier with Dan overhead to help move the cattle along. He was worth four men on horseback.

She admired the energetic way he attacked his job, as well. The men had taken to him easily, and he had taken charge of his duties on the ranch with gusto.

It was a godsend to have such a good crew working under her when she had so many other worries on her mind. Pettigrew hadn't been easy to deal with this past week. He had barraged her with phone calls, demanding restitution for his cattle and protesting his innocence regarding their straying onto her land. As far as he was concerned, the Bar T owed him for the cattle no matter what killed them or where it came from. They were on her land when they died, and that was that.

It didn't help that the samples Doc Hollander sent to the state lab were still being analyzed. She didn't know what was taking them so long but felt it couldn't be good.

Jo was beginning to agree with Dan by this time. She'd rather have a full-blown range war than suffer one more phone call from her irate neighbor. She had the air power, after all.

She watched the helicopter wheel around overhead, a swiftly moving black spot against the bright blue sky. He flew magnificently, the helicopter like an extension of his body. Though she hadn't allowed herself to be talked into another ride, she was now convinced that he was the man she'd want at the controls should she ever need to fly again.

Thinking about Dan made Jo feel happy and secure. The problem with Pettigrew faded behind the image of Dan's smiling face. She had found over the past couple days that nearly every thought faded in comparison to thoughts of Dan. So self-assured, yet modest. So handsome...

Her thoughts ranged further afield every time she thought of him until they began to embarrass her slightly, and she had to will herself to concentrate on other tasks. Still, he remained in the back of her mind, a picture of his face instantly available whenever his voice cut through the static on the radio.

And, as a bonus, he had also proven that he could cook. His meat loaf was excellent—just as he had promised.

"Hey, flyboy," she called over the radio, using the nickname that had settled on him over his week of flying the herd. "Bring her on down to roost. We're going out on the town tonight. Over."

"I don't know, Jo," came his reply. "It's been a long day. Over."

"Boss's orders," she called back. "All work and no play makes for ornery cowboys. Come on down and wash up. Over."

"Roger, boss. Over and out."

Jo smiled. It was about time she brought him to town. They'd been so busy with the cattle that no one had been out all week, and now they all felt like kicking up their heels a bit. Besides, she was still curious about his dancing. She wanted to find out if Dan danced as well as he flew.

DAN SMILED as he swept his helicopter around in a descending arc over Pettigrew land and then east toward the Bar T ranch house. Many of his hours aloft had been spent in contemplation of his lithe young boss—a mental tug-of-war between his obligation to her as an employer and his growing desire for her as a woman.

Joanne Tate was about as perfect a woman as Dan could ever imagine meeting. That was a fact that had become more than evident over the course of a week when his feelings had grown from simple infatuation to something more. If she weren't his boss, he would have asked her out days ago.

He had never been in a position where he was so unsure of himself. But, rather than feeling uncomfortable, he felt strangely happy. Just being near Jo brought on that happiness. Just hearing her voice over the radio.

Turning the aircraft toward home, he noticed a truck proceeding along a gravel road on Pettigrew's land. He might not have paid any attention to it except that it didn't appear to be a cattle truck or any other type of farm truck. He was too far away to really see it, however, and rather than try to get a closer look, he continued making his way back to the Bar T. It wasn't on Tate land, after all, so it really wasn't any of his business.

WHILE DAN WAS FLYING home and the rest of the crew was returning on horseback, a solitary figure was making his way through the Tate house. He had entered through the unlocked kitchen door and moved swiftly through the late Jonas Tate's den and to the gun cabinet within.

The man paused at the cabinet, stooping to examine the lock before selecting a slender pick to work it open. The ornate lock, built more for style than function, gave way easily, and the man carefully opened the door with one gloved hand.

It only took a moment for him to remove a shotgun from the stand of hunting rifles and close the cabinet again. He relocked the door and then hurried away, slipping out the kitchen door and over the rise to his waiting horse well before anyone returned to the ranch.

"DANIEL, this is Mary Montgomery."

Jo stood up from the table she, Dan and Hank had taken at Northern Lights, the main night spot in the modest community of Oak River. Smiling broadly, she pulled the petite redhead over to their table.

Dan couldn't help but notice how Hank had looked down at the table when Mary came up to them, noticing, too, that Mary's eyes couldn't seem to stay off the foreman.

"Mary is my oldest friend in the world," Jo said. "Mary, Daniel is my new helicopter pilot."

"Glad to meet you," the young woman said as she accepted a chair at the table. "I heard that Jo was moving into the modern world, but I didn't hear she was looking for anyone so handsome. I'd have come out to visit if I had. You're her new one-man roundup crew?"

"Well, I can't rope them from the air, but we're gonna try to give those cow ponies a rest," Dan said.

"You'll have to bring him to town more often, Jo," Mary said. "Don't keep him all to yourself out there."

"Maybe I had better," Jo replied. Mary's attention to Dan made her feel slightly, inexplicably angry. She had expected better of Mary, but should have known she would put on an act with Hank, her ex-beau, at the table.

Dan didn't know how to react to the woman. He wasn't entirely at ease dealing with new people in a social situation, and he wasn't sure how he was supposed to act with this woman who Jo obviously liked a great deal. The whole evening was a bit awkward for him so far. He'd been working in the city too long and had forgotten that Westerners tended to play as hard as they worked.

"How was your first week?" Mary asked. She sipped from a glass of beer, eyeing him with naked speculation.

"I'm working at getting Jo used to flying," he answered. He glanced at his employer then, smiling. "She's a tough sell."

"She's been up with you?" Mary laughed, shaking her long red hair back happily. "She used to get sick on the merry-go-round," she said.

"I did not!"

"And every summer when the carnival came around, we had to drag her, kicking and screaming, onto the roller coaster."

"She did very well," Dan said. "We'll be ready to start lessons any day."

"I'd pay to see Jo fly a helicopter," Mary said. "So, how did you manage to get her up?"

"She was in a hurry," he said. "Had to take a look at some cattle."

"I heard about that," Mary commented, nodding. "You've got Norton Pettigrew about to bust a vein."

"I wish he would and get it over with," Jo said, beginning to push her chair back from the table. "But, hey, we're not supposed to be working tonight. We came here to relax."

"He looks relaxed," Mary said, leaning toward Dan and placing one hand on his shoulder. "Do you dance?"

"He's a Texan," Hank said, slapping Dan on the back. "Of course he dances."

"It's been a while," Dan admitted.

"Well, the band will be back on stage in a couple minutes," Mary said. "I hope your employer isn't planning to monopolize your time."

"Oh, come on, I didn't hire him to dance with me," Jo protested, good-naturedly. She inched her chair up a bit to cover the earlier movement. "Dan can dance with anybody he wants to. But I thought you and Ken were getting serious."

"I don't know where Ken is, and I'm in the mood for dancing," the other woman said. "I'm not going to wait for him to show up."

"Watch out for her," Hank told Dan. "She'll wear you out before the night is through."

"I'm really not much of a dancer," Dan said. "I'm sure Hank would like to take a turn on the floor."

"I grew up dancing with Hank," Mary said flatly. "The thrill is gone, darlin'."

Hank laughed, settling back in his chair, but the laugh was short-lived, and hard-sounding, a fact that Dan couldn't help but notice. Jo noticed it, too, and wondered how wise it was to have dropped Dan into the local scene without first supplying him with some vital details. Hank and Mary had been an item not too long ago, and their split had not been Hank's idea. The foreman was still in the thrall of the teasing young redhead, and he was just the type of hotheaded cowboy who would hold a grudge. And, for that matter, Ken Zane, Mary's current beau, wasn't known for his easygoing disposition, either. It seemed that Zane, who had blown into town a couple months ago selling farm chemicals and seed, had decided to put down roots in town. He had also, apparently, decided that Mary Montgomery was the best person in town to spend time with.

It would be just like Mary to be playing Dan as some sort of pawn in her own love life, and Jo could only hope she wasn't doing it now. She felt a protectiveness toward Dan that she didn't normally feel toward new employees, and she didn't want to see him hurt.

The band was returning to the stage just then, so she didn't suppose there was much chance of rescuing him at the moment. It would look odd to everyone if she tried. All she could hope was that their turn on the dance floor would be through before Ken arrived and complicated Dan's first visit to town.

"Well," she said. "I see that your big chance has come, Mary. Maybe I'll let him have one dance before I get him out of your clutches."

"One chance is all I need," Mary replied with a sugary drawl. "It's about time we got some new blood in this tired old town."

"Howdy," the man on the stage shouted out over the microphone, cutting off their conversation. "You folks have been dancing up a storm tonight, and we sure appreciate it. The management has asked us to remind you that Bob Barnes will be back all next week. They'd like y'all down here on Saturday for the line dance. Meantime, we're the Montana Rovers, and we're here through Friday night, so y'all come back and see us before we go. We're going to start out with what the rock-and-roll stations would call a few 'golden oldies'. You fellas grab your best gal and get out on the floor to dance the 'Tennessee Waltz.'"

The band started playing the classic song, and Mary jumped to her feet and grabbed Dan's arm. "Come on, cowboy, here's your chance to dance with the prettiest woman in Oak River."

Dan stood, looking toward Jo as if hoping for some excuse not to dance; but he let himself be pulled onto the floor with the other couples who had begun moving to the strains of the time-honored melody.

Jo watched them, feeling vaguely put out by her friend's behavior at claiming Dan's company. She'd clearly had too much to drink, Jo felt, but even sober it was very much like her to swoop in on any new, good-looking man. Jo had never liked that in the past, and she liked it even less now.

Relax girl, he's your employee, she thought. But, now that she saw them moving together, their bodies close and their arms around each other, she felt a bit jealous. No, she felt a great deal jealous, and it came as a surprise to her.

Hank was watching them, too, his eyes narrowed as he chugged his bottle of beer. It was clear to Jo that he still had feelings for the comely woman, deep feelings. It wouldn't do for him to start feeling enmity toward Dan because of Mary's machinations.

"They dance good together," Hank said, turning pointedly away from the dance floor to look at Jo.

"They do," Jo agreed curtly. She wondered if her jealousy was as visible as Hank's was. "I wish Mary would drink less."

"She's not drunk," Hank said. "She's just playing her games. She's hoping that idiot she's hooked up with now will walk in and make a fuss. Poor Danny walked right into it, too."

"No, we pushed him into it," Jo said. "I should have filled him in before taking him out for a night on the town. A person could get hurt walking into a situation like this blind."

"He's a big boy."

Hank's eyes wandered from Jo's face for a moment, a smile flickering across his lips as he watched the door. Jo was watching the dancers, however, and didn't see his reaction to the tall newcomer who was looking over the patrons of the bar in search of his woman.

"What are you looking at?" Jo turned, scanning the people behind her quickly, missing the man who was now moving rapidly through the crowd.

"Thought I saw someone to dance with," he said casually.

Then Jo saw Ken Zane as he walked past the tables and onto the dance floor with his fists balled at his sides and an angry look on his face. She stood, about to shout a warning, but he'd already gotten to them by then.

Ken tapped Dan on the shoulder like any man looking to cut in would do, and Dan turned with a somewhat relieved look on his face. But, instead of asking for a turn with the other man's partner, Ken snapped his fist out squarely against Dan's cheek and sent him sprawling on his back amid the startled dancers.

"Oh, hell," Jo exclaimed, starting toward the two men in the center of a suddenly very empty dance floor.

But, before she could make her move to stop any further violence, Dan had snapped up to his feet almost as quickly as he had fallen. In one seemingly effortless move, he jumped and spun, catching Ken in the side of the head with the blurred motion of his foot. As the man staggered back, Dan spun and swept his other foot across the back of Ken's knees. Then he grasped one of Ken's arms, propelling him to his stomach on the floor with his hand twisted up behind his head.

Jo hadn't even taken two steps in the time it took Dan to subdue his attacker, and she stopped and stared at them in wonderment.

"So, who the hell are you?" Dan asked, kneeling on the man's back. "And could you please tell me why you're trying to get me to bust you up?"

The man on the floor didn't say anything, but Mary cut in with an explanation.

"That's Ken," Mary exclaimed, excitedly. "He's a little hotheaded."

Mary was flushed, smiling, and clearly in as much awe of Dan's defensive maneuver as Jo was. This wasn't what Jo had expected, but she was definitely pleased with it.

"You own this guy?" Dan asked Mary contemptuously. "Well, you should put him on a shorter leash."

Dan stood up and backed away, keeping his eyes on the man who rolled and sat rubbing the side of his head as Mary knelt beside him. The two men stared at each other for a moment, then Ken smiled slyly, his eyes still riveted on Dan's face. Taking his smile as their cue, people began moving and talking again. The band started playing another song as Mary helped Ken to his feet, kissing the side of his face where he'd been wounded in battle for her.

Dan walked toward Jo, a pensive look on his face. He smiled as he reached her, however. "Interesting town you've got here, boss," he said, leaning toward her to be heard over the band. He picked up his glass of beer from the table and drained what was left in it.

"It may be more interesting now that you're here," she replied. "Would you like to go now?"

"No," he said resolutely. "You know I can't just up and leave. It would let him save face."

"What's wrong with that?"

"He's trouble," Dan said. "Not as much trouble as his girlfriend, I don't suppose, but trouble, anyway. A man can't back away from trouble."

"Men have too many rules."

"Of course, there's a more important reason why I want to stay," he said. Placing one hand on her shoulder, he leaned close to her face and smiled. "I can't leave because I haven't danced with my boss, yet."

"Oh, well that's a reason I can understand."

"Shall we?" He offered her his arm with a slight bow.

"I would love to."

Jo accepted his arm and walked onto the floor with him where they began moving to the tempo of another country waltz. His arm felt good—strong—across her back, and his hand holding hers was broad and capable. He danced naturally well, leading her around the floor with the same ease he'd shown in besting Mary's beau. And, as he danced, he held her close and kept his eyes on hers, as though she was the most interesting woman on the planet and dancing with her was the most pleasant experience he could imagine.

"This is better," he said. "Your friend isn't a very good dancer."

"Really? I always thought she was good. Men like dancing with her, anyway." Mary had certainly never lacked partners, in Jo's experience.

"I'm sure they do," he said, grinning. "She dances like she wants sex."

"What?" His reply surprised her. "How do you do that?"

"She doesn't dance, she rubs up against you like a cat looking for a meal."

"And how do I dance?"

"You dance like you want to dance," he told her. "And you do it very well."

"Well," Jo said. "I do think its only proper that I remain somewhat businesslike." She did enjoy this man. He was honest and witty and not afraid to say what was on his mind. She enjoyed that a great deal in a man.

"Well, I suppose it's businesslike, boss," he said. "But you still manage to get a man interested."

Jo laughed and let that stand as her reply, but she allowed herself the unbusinesslike luxury of placing her cheek against his chest as they continued dancing. She closed her eyes, enjoying the warmth of his body next to hers as she let him pilot them around the dance floor for this and many dances to come.

While they danced, Ken Zane kept his eye on them, a small, bitter smile playing at his lips. He seemed to be measuring Dan, gauging his weaknesses and strengths for a further encounter. Ken was not the type of man to take defeat lightly.

Mary danced with him happily, unaware of his scrutiny of Dan, because her own attention was on Hank, seated sourly at the bar and watching them with open animosity. She smiled at him, causing him to turn away rather than smile in return.

In the break between songs, a man entered the bar and swiftly approached Zane. He whispered something in Ken's ear, causing him to smile for the first time in hours. Only when the man left did he return his attention to Mary, relaxing as though he hadn't a care in the world.

Life couldn't be sweeter for Ken Zane than it was right then. And when life was sweet for Zane, it was usually miserable for somebody else.

Chapter Four

It was well after midnight when Dan and Jo left the bar. Neither had very much to drink over the course of the evening—they'd been too busy dancing—but still Jo drove her elderly Cadillac slowly and carefully along the dirt road toward home. She drove with the top down, enjoying the wind moving through her hair. She was pleasantly tired and eager for bed, yet she found that she was enjoying Dan's company so much, she didn't want to drive any faster.

The stars twinkled brightly overhead, a sight that Dan couldn't seem to get enough of as they drove. "This is beautiful," he said. "I've been in the city too long. You can't see the stars beyond the city lights. It gives a person an exaggerated sense of their own importance when they can't see the stars."

"Feeling philosophical tonight, are you?" Jo drove with one hand, dividing her attention between the empty road and the man sitting beside her with his head resting on the back of the seat as he watched the stars overhead. "You're a different kind of cowhand, that's for sure."

"I hope that's good," he said, sitting up straight as he looked over at her with rapt concentration.

"It's good," Jo told him. "My father used to drive me out to the middle of the ranch in the dead of night in this old car. He'd park on one of the access roads and show me the constellations."

"Could have done it from your back porch," Dan commented. "It can't be that much lighter there."

"No, but I think he just liked to come out in the middle of all this land just to get the feel of it beneath the stars. You're right. The stars give you a whole different sense of proportion."

"So stop the car," he suggested. "Show me your stars."

Jo smiled, thinking of the absurdity of looking at the stars with her hired help on a warm summer night. But then she did pull over and stop, and the stillness of the prairie seemed to rush in on them when the engine of the big car was silenced.

"It's been a long time since I looked at the stars," Jo said. "I don't really remember them."

"Any names we might give them don't really matter, anyway," Dan said. He settled back in his seat once more, looking up at the universe around them. "The stars don't care what we call them."

"No, and we're just a speck among them." Jo slipped down behind the wheel, resting her head on the back of her seat and watching the twinkling show. "That's what my dad used to say. In daylight the ranch seemed to be the whole world, but it just disappeared at night. I wish I could remember their names, though."

"Well, there's Virgo over there," he said.

"Where?"

"Over there." He moved nearer on the seat and placed one hand on her shoulder and pointed with the other so that she could sight along his arm toward the constellation. "See it?"

"Yes, I remember." His hand was warm on her shoulder, warmer than the night air, and she found herself feeling slightly dizzy all of a sudden. "And that's Ursa Major up there, right?"

"Yes, that's it. You do too remember."

"How do you know them? Navigational aids?"

"No, army pilots navigate by computer," he said, taking his hand away. "I used to read a lot."

"Used to?" Her shoulder felt cold without his hand there, and she shivered slightly.

"I can't pack much of a library into a helicopter."

"No, I wouldn't suppose you can. What about that little show in the bar? You didn't learn that in books."

Jo turned toward him, somewhat startled to see that though he had removed his hand, he hadn't moved away on the seat of the car, and his face was now only inches from hers.

"I used to get beat up a lot as a kid," he admitted. "After I studied martial arts, I didn't get beat up anymore."

"Do you have a belt of some kind?" She didn't know anything about martial arts beyond what she'd seen in a few movies and TV shows.

"Black belt in karate and tae kwan do. Actually, what I studied was a sort of hybrid that some people call American karate. There's not much philosophy to it except to hit back harder than they hit you. Appropriate force."

"I'd always thought martial arts were about breaking boards and that sort of thing. I never thought that all the stuff they do in the movies was anywhere near the real thing."

"Well, the quickest way to stop somebody from attacking you is to break a bone or two," Dan said. "That's where all that board busting comes in."

"Oh, so that's just showing off."

"Something like that," he replied. "So, what's the deal with that Zane fella?"

"I'm not sure about him," Jo said. "He sells farm chemicals, seeds and a few other things, but he must not have much of a territory because he's always in town. And he never tried selling me anything at the Bar T. As near as I can tell, Pettigrew is his primary customer around here, because he's always going out there."

Jo was talking without really paying attention to her words. All she could concentrate on just then was the faint glimmer of starlight on her companion's eyes and the soft shadows the pale light created in his cheeks. He was there, near enough for her to touch him or for him to touch her, and she found herself wanting to be touched. Contrary to any acceptable form of behavior and every ideal she'd ever sought for her own behavior, all she wanted to do was to lie in his arms and watch the stars while the gentle murmur of his voice soothed her ears.

Dan cleared his throat, moving just slightly back from her.

"I didn't really want to go dancing tonight," he said. "I'm not good with crowds."

"You didn't have to go," she said. "I just thought you might like to get out and sample Oak River's social life."

"I'm glad I went. I enjoyed myself. Or, I should say that you made it easy to enjoy myself."

"Good."

"I like you, Joanne Tate," he said, knowing that every word he uttered would drag him deeper into the possibility of trouble. He couldn't help himself, though, for the woman beside him was too special to let it go without acknowledging it. "You're a fine woman, and I can't think of anyone I'd rather have for a boss."

"I've never liked the word *boss*," she said softly.

"Neither have I, before now."

He knew he could kiss her and find some excuse for it if she objected. If he leaned toward her ever so slightly, he could put his lips to hers before she might stop him, but their relationship was too new and too oddly formal for such forwardness. He wasn't sure what he should do and was afraid of what he would do.

"You should just call me Jo like everyone else," she said. "*Boss* is too overbearing a word for me."

"You're definitely not overbearing."

Jo could see how his eyes were roving over her face, studying everything at once as he sat so near and spoke to her. She could see his dilemma, see him wanting to make contact as badly as she did, but not knowing how to go about it with his employer. His clear desire gave her a tingle of anticipation. She knew that when he did overcome his awkwardness, his kiss would be wonderful.

"You haven't had any second thoughts about the job, have you?" she said.

"No. In fact, I was just thinking I might work here forever."

"That's a long time."

"Maybe not long enough."

And they began to move together, without thought or intention, and then stopped in the same manner, their lips inches apart. A palpable sense of yearning hung between them, drawing them together like a magnetic attraction, even while the circumstances of their relationship held them apart. She was his employer and so he should not attempt a kiss, should not feel the way he felt just then; and it was improper for Jo to seem to be forcing a kiss upon him. Reluctantly, they slipped away from the tempting union of their lips and turned their eyes away from each other.

Jo's heart was pounding so hard that she was sure he could hear it as clearly as she could. She felt flushed, hot within her clothing as her desire became a need that she had to fight against to keep from throwing her arms around him.

How could this feeling have overcome her so rapidly? Was one week enough time to feel the way she did? All she knew was the impropriety of her feelings and the fact that she had to fight against them. For now, at least, she would fight against them.

The gravelly sound of an approaching vehicle broke the tension that was growing around them. The bright glare of lights bounced over the countryside until Hank Driscoll's Jeep bounded past with a jaunty sounding of its horn. The taillights rose and then dipped below the next hill, leaving them alone again.

"Maybe it's time we headed on back, boss," Dan offered, turning his hat slowly around in his lap.

"Like I said before, there's no need to be formal. Everyone calls me Jo." She started the engine and slipped the car into gear to continue moving along the road toward the ranch. After a moment, to calm her breathing, she said, "I think we should continue our discussion at a later time."

"I'd like that," he said. "When there's time for a complete discussion."

"Right." Jo grinned, hoping he couldn't see her smile. "And privacy."

"Oh, yes, definitely more privacy." He didn't say anything for a short while, then turned toward her. "I really enjoyed dancing with you, Jo. Would you do me the honor of accompanying me to the dance this Saturday night?"

"I'd be honored," she replied as they rose over the hill and began their descent. She could see Hanks' taillights ahead of them, apparently stopped near the rise of the next hill.

"Is your foreman waiting to check up on us? We haven't broken curfew, have we?"

Jo had seen the lights ahead of them, too. The car was definitely parked, and they could see Hank standing beside the road as they neared him.

"I should warn you about Hank," she said. "Especially since I didn't think to warn you about Mary. He's likely to give you a hard time if he thinks there's something between us. Nothing bad, you know, but he's a natural kidder. He probably will, anyway, since you're new, but especially if he thinks you're moving a little too fast on the boss."

"Am I? Moving too fast, I mean," Dan asked. "I didn't mean to, but it just seemed to happen."

"No," she assured him as she slowed the car and stopped behind Hank's Jeep. "You're not moving too fast at all."

"You better get up here, Jo," Hank called to them. "We've got trouble here."

"More cattle?" Jo and Dan hurried from the car to see what the foreman was looking at on the roadside.

"Worse than that."

Jo gasped when she saw the object of Hank's concern. The body of a middle-aged man lay faceup in the grass along the gravel road, blood saturating the ground around him and spattered on his face.

"Is he dead?" she asked.

"Shot in the head it looks like," Hank said. "I didn't touch him."

"Do you know who he is?" Dan knelt beside the body but didn't touch it. There was obviously no point in touching him now. "Does he work for you?"

"No, he doesn't work for me," Jo said stonily. "That's Norton Pettigrew."

Chapter Five

"So, this is—or rather, was—Norton Pettigrew?" Dan continued to crouch beside the body, examining it for a moment in the moonlight. "Do you have a flashlight?"

"Yes," Jo said. "Why?"

"I think it would be in your interest to see if there are any clues at the crime scene," Dan told her. "Hank, can you run in for the sheriff? I imagine it would look better if there were two people here with the body rather than one."

"Yeah," the other man said. "I suppose you're right on that. It'll take me about ten minutes, I suspect. No more than that."

"Great." Dan stood up and thrust his hands into the front pockets of his jeans. "We'll be waiting."

Hank returned to his vehicle and used the opposite shoulder of the road to turn around and head back to town. After he'd gone, Dan walked with Jo to her car.

"Did you tell Hank about any of your phone conversations with Pettigrew?" he asked her.

"Yes, I believe I mentioned them," she said as she opened the glove box and took out a flashlight. "Why?"

"I didn't know if you'd told anyone. If you hadn't, I'd have advised keeping it to yourself." He accepted the flashlight from her.

"It's not as though people don't know what little regard I had for him," Jo said as they walked back to the body. "But I'm hardly the only one to be on the outs with Pettigrew."

"Well, somebody was more out than most, I'd say." Dan stood over the body and directed the beam of the flashlight down at it. "I guess they didn't want to wait and settle things in court."

"What are we looking for?"

"I don't know." Dan let the light wander over the man's rumpled and dusty suit. "But it can't hurt to look, can it?"

"Are we allowed to snoop like this?"

"It's your land." He crouched carefully. "Just don't move anything." Then he leaned closer, looking at Pettigrew's left hip, which was upturned slightly. "Or, don't move too many things," he revised. "He was left-handed?"

"Yes." Jo crouched beside him to see what he was looking at. Pettigrew's wallet was protruding from the left hip pocket of his pants; it had been exposed because his suit coat had slid up when he fell.

"You're not going to pick his pocket, are you? Goodness, Dan, I know that's not legal."

"Of course I'm going to pick his pocket. He's not going to mind a bit. Here, hold this." He handed her the flashlight, which she took without protest. "Aim the light on the pocket so I can get the wallet out without messing things up."

"Please, Dan," she said, though she didn't make a move to stop him.

"They wouldn't have killed him on your land if they didn't want you blamed for it. And, if that's the case, we'd better do our best to be certain they didn't plant anything on Pettigrew to incriminate you." Dan spoke grimly as he reached for the billfold.

Jo trained the light on the wallet without saying anything else while Dan worked it free. She admired the way he'd assessed the situation and taken action. There was no holding back with this man, no indecisiveness, and that appealed to her. The idea of being caught going through the dead man's wallet didn't appeal to her, however, no matter how prudent it might be to do so. When he got the wallet out and sat back on his haunches with it, she let a long sigh of relief escape her lips and brought the light to bear on the billfold.

"Over two hundred dollars," Dan said, fanning the bills with his thumb without removing them from the wallet. "Credit cards, identification. All still here. Here we go." He removed several business cards and a sheet of folded notepaper from the credit-card slot in the wallet and began sorting through them. "Stop me if you see anything unusual in this stuff," he said to Jo. "Looks like he kept every salesman's card that ever got handed to him."

"None of them are out of the ordinary so far," she commented as she watched him slowly go through the papers in the wallet. "Seed and chemical dealers, cattle auctions. Pretty ordinary. Wait," she said, stopping him with a hand on his arm. "New Jersey? What's he doing with the business card of a chemical dealer from New Jersey? He wouldn't need anything that he couldn't get locally."

"This is a chemical hauler, a guy who disposes of chemicals," Dan said. "James Chemicals, Trenton,

New Jersey. Might just be one of many salesmen look-ing for a commission in the wrong place,'' he said as he sorted the card to the bottom of the stack and unfolded the sheet of notepaper. "But we'll keep it in mind.''

"Phone numbers,'' Jo commented at his side as she read the notations. "I'll get some paper.''

"I've got some here,'' Dan said before she could rise. He took a leather-bound notepad from his hip pocket and flipped it open. "I keep a log of air time,'' he ex-plained as he folded back several pages of scribbled notes to expose a clean sheet. He secured the sheet of phone numbers against his knee and copied them quickly.

"Hurry,'' Jo said as he refolded the paper and slipped it to the bottom of the stack again. Then Dan put the cards back into the wallet and carefully replaced it in the dead man's pocket.

"Boy, I sure wouldn't make it as a criminal,'' Jo said. "I'm nervous as a cat.''

"Me, too,'' Dan admitted. "What kind of finger-print equipment does your sheriff have?''

"Why?''

"Well, if he wants to get picky about it, he'll be able to get a whole bunch of my prints off the wallet now. I'm assuming that he's not awfully picky.''

"You don't think he'll check, do you?''

"Hope not,'' Dan said. "But there's no sense wor-rying about that now.''

"Is there anything else to be gained here? Can't we just wait by the car until the sheriff comes?'' Jo asked. She was anxious to get away from the body now and not linger so close to death. "I'm not real comfortable with any of this.''

"No, I don't suppose there's anything here that the law can't discover for themselves. It looks like his killer shot him from that side." He pointed to the other side of the body as he stood. "It doesn't look like he spun after being shot since his coat slid straight up behind him rather than twisted around him like it would've if he'd spun. Besides, the spattered blood seems to be on this side of the body."

"Okay, that's enough for me," Jo said, standing. "Let's go wait by the car now."

"Good idea."

They walked to the car, leaned against the fender and stared at the body lying in the pale moonlight. The Montana landscape spread out around them, a vast and empty scene of gently rolling hills rising in the distance and lit in shades of blue and gray by the moon. Under other circumstances, it would have been a very romantic scene. Tonight it only served to make Jo feel cold. The land was too vast, too distant from human concerns—and death was far too near.

Jo found herself instinctively moving closer to the tall man at her side for warmth, and she was glad when he put his arm around her shoulder and held her without a word as though he, too, felt the lonely chill that had overcome the evening.

"So," he said after a moment. "Who else hated Norton Pettigrew?"

"Hated? Well, even I didn't hate him," she said. "I just didn't have much use for him."

"But who would want to kill him?"

"God, I don't know." She sighed, trying vainly to think of anyone she knew who would go to such extremes to settle a score with the rancher. "Nobody that I can think of," she admitted at last.

"Okay, so who might not mind killing Pettigrew if they could manage to get you arrested for the murder?"

"You mean kill him specifically to frame me?"

"Two birds with one stone," Dan said.

"I don't have any enemies."

"Well, maybe not, but the closest thing you had to an enemy is lying dead on your grazing land just a week after ten of his cattle turned up dead on your land. It's going to look mighty suspicious to the law, unless we can keep the cattle out of it."

"Fat chance," Jo said ruefully. "Evan Hollander, the vet you met last week, is the sheriff's uncle."

"Okay, so it looks like the sheriff already has the beginning of a motive. You should get in touch with your lawyer in the morning."

"Why on earth would I need my lawyer? I haven't done anything. I wasn't even here when he was killed."

"Sure, but you wouldn't have done it personally, would you? You don't have to have been here at the time."

"I don't pay any of my men enough to commit murder," Jo protested. "Not even if one of them was capable of murder."

"Okay, so you're innocent as a newborn babe and have nothing to fear." Dan laughed, tightening his arm around Jo's shoulder. "Optimism is a charming attribute, boss, but the law has a funny way of wanting to pin murders on somebody. They might overlook you at first, but if they can't find anyone else, they'll come around again."

"If we cooperate with the sheriff, we should be able to figure out who killed him, Daniel," Jo said. "There aren't that many candidates to choose from."

"Which is why they did their best to put you at the top of the list," Dan said. "You can cooperate with the law till hell freezes over, but it won't help if you remain the most logical suspect. I would suggest that we check things out on our own and see what we can come up with. That way, we'll be one up on them if they try pinning it on you."

"There's no point in that. Andrew Hollander is an intelligent man. He'll look at the facts fairly."

"I don't doubt that for a minute," he said, turning his head to look back along the road behind them. "It looks like we're going to have our chance to check out his fair-mindedness right now."

Jo followed his gaze along the road. A red light flashed a ways up. The sheriff was racing toward them fast enough to raise a cloud of dust that was visible even in the moonlight. Behind him they could see the lights of two other vehicles, as well.

Dan gave Jo a reassuring squeeze with his arm, and then stepped away before the lights of the approaching cars could illuminate them.

Jo couldn't help but smile at the way in which he had moved his arm away to avoid giving anyone a false impression about them. She had known plenty of men who would have wanted to stake a claim on her by remaining as close as possible for all to see. Men like that, possessors, had never gotten far with her. No, but a gentleman like Dan, one who sought to maintain her position no matter what bragging rights he might gain by proximity, was someone Jo could really fall for. In fact, she felt sure that she already had.

But grim reality intervened into her thoughts as the sheriff's car stopped by hers. A moment later, Hank's vehicle stopped behind his, followed by another car that she didn't recognize in the dim light.

Sheriff Andrew Hollander got out of the car and hitched his gun belt up over his hips before walking toward Jo and Dan. Glen Wright, his deputy, got out of the car that was parked behind Hank's vehicle and hurried to join them in a shuffling sort of trot. Though Andrew was only two years his deputy's senior, it was clear from his demeanor who was the man in command. Where Andrew ambled, Glen scampered, and Andrew's measured tone of voice was stridently offset by Glen's nervous bark. Glen would always be a deputy, that much was certain when seen beside his boss.

Away from Andrew, however, Glen's attitude hardened. His apparent need to please was gone, replaced by an assertion of authority far beyond his job as deputy sheriff. Because of this, most people who had any need of the law were content to bide their time rather than take the problem to Glen. And that was why Jo was glad to see that Andrew had been available to handle the matter tonight.

"'Evening, Jo," Andrew said as he walked up to the pair. "Got trouble, eh?"

"Looks like," she replied. "I don't know what to make of it."

"Well, let's take a look and see what there is." He walked a few feet past them and stared at the body for a moment and then turned to Dan. "And you are...?" he asked.

"Dan Fitzpatrick." Dan met the sheriff's stare evenly and calmly.

"The pilot?"

"That's right."

"Hank found the body?" Andrew asked Jo.

"Yes, he passed us on the road just a moment or two before coming upon it."

"Is this exactly the way you found it, Hank?"

Sheriff Hollander motioned toward the body at the edge of the road as he looked toward Hank, who was waiting by his car. The foreman walked up beside Jo's car to get a better look and then nodded, saying, "Yes, it doesn't look like it's been moved any."

"Good." The sheriff took another couple steps toward the body, then paused again. "Any of you folks touch the corpse?"

"No," Hank said.

"I did," Dan answered. "He looked dead, but I figured we should be certain."

"Sensible," Andrew commented as he continued toward the body and crouched beside it to play the beam of his flashlight over the still form. Glen walked a bit farther along the side of the road and then down, shuffling his feet as he approached the body behind the sheriff.

"So, had you and Norton been arguing pretty steady lately, Jo?" Andrew asked without looking at her.

"Well, I guess so," she said. "Is that much different from usual?"

Jo had been somewhat shocked by the question and equally shocked by the apparent calm in her voice when she answered him. She hadn't expected his questions to turn so quickly to the matter of the cattle—she thought he'd linger on the physical facts of the matter first—so when he jumped right to the question of motive in such a personal manner, she was taken aback.

"He's been after my uncle about the results all week," Andrew said. Then he smiled slightly. "Evan is about at the point where he'd make a pretty good suspect in this thing if he owned a shotgun.''

"Yes, well, lots of people have been inches away from killing Norton over the years but haven't done it," she said.

"Somebody finally went the distance."

"How soon does Evan expect to hear about the cattle?"

"Couple days more," Andrew replied. "You folks didn't touch his wallet, did you?"

"Sure," Dan said quickly. "I took fifty bucks out to pay for the emotional distress of seeing him like this."

"You can that crap!" Glen snapped, taking one threatening step toward Dan. "The sheriff is conducting an investigation here."

But the sheriff was chuckling quietly. "Relax, Glen, I wasn't all that serious. It's just one of those questions they say you have to ask when a body's wallet is so clearly exposed, and there's a fair number of footprints near the body."

"I told you I touched the body," Dan said. "I didn't walk on the other side of him, though, and it looks like the shot came from that side."

"Just how do you know that?" Glen asked quickly, stepping toward the pilot.

"The blood is splattered on the other side, is how," Dan said. "Like the murderer was on the other side and standing a bit closer to the road when he fired."

"And you're an expert?" Glen asked.

"I know one end of a gun from another," Dan answered. "But I don't suppose that makes me an expert."

"No, I don't suppose it does," Glen said in dismissal.

"You're probably right, though," Andrew said as he came back up toward the road. "I'd say the killer was standing right about where my deputy was dragging his feet a few minutes ago."

Though Andrew spoke in a conversational manner, it was clear from Glen's stiffening posture that the rebuke had hit home. Once it had, however, Glen merely tightened his gaze on Dan's face as though blaming him for his own inept treatment of the crime scene.

"Where did you walk when you were here, Hank?" Glen asked.

"Straight down toward his feet and around the left there," he answered, indicating the side on which Dan had crouched beside the body.

"Okay," Andrew said, "I don't see much else for you folks to do here. We're going to rope off the scene. That'll include the road, Jo, so use the other entrance for a day or two, okay?"

"Fine."

"I'll let you go now."

"Thank you, Sheriff," Dan said, turning toward him in a way that made it obvious he was excluding Glen from any thanks he might have.

"Right." Andrew extended his hand to Dan. "It was a pleasure meeting you, no matter the circumstances. My uncle says you're offering helicopter rides."

"Sure am." Dan grinned. "Have you been up in one before?"

"No."

"All the better," Dan answered. "I'll give you a ride to remember."

"Yes, I bet you will at that."

"I THINK THE SHERIFF likes me," Dan said as they drove toward the ranch compound. But he wasn't smiling as he spoke, and his eyes were narrowed in concentration. "Of course, the deputy hates my guts."

"You didn't seem to hit it off very well there, no. But he isn't always very friendly, anyway," Jo stated. "He's touchy sometimes. Especially after he messes up a crime scene."

"He was a bit sloppy about that. Is he normally so slipshod?"

"I don't know." Jo slowed and turned the car into the front yard. "He's a moody fellow, not normally lax, I don't think. But then, he was at the bar tonight."

"That probably explains it," Dan said as the car stopped. He remained seated for a moment even as Jo opened her door and got out.

"What's wrong?" she asked.

"I don't know." Then he shrugged, smiling. "Probably nothing at all," he admitted as he got out of the car. "It's just that something is bugging me, and I can't put my finger on it."

"Don't try so hard," Jo advised. She stretched, throwing her arms back to work the kinks out of her body as she stood by the car. "Maybe you'd like to come in for a moment."

"Yes, I would," Dan said. "But I should probably head out to the bunkhouse and get some sleep."

"Oh, I guess that would be a good idea." Still, Jo felt disappointed that he wouldn't be coming in. She enjoyed his company and had hoped to have a chance to unwind a bit after the horrifying end their evening had come to. "Get some rest. We need to start moving the rest of the herd in from the north range in the morning."

"Right, boss," he said with a grin. "You get some rest, yourself. Good night."

Jo watched him walk into the darkness beyond the porch, listening to the crunch of the footsteps that carried him to the pool of light in front of the bunkhouse. She continued watching as he opened the door and went inside, then she turned and entered her own home.

Her house seemed strangely empty tonight.

Chapter Six

The next morning was cloudless with a sky of pristine, blistering blue in which the sun glowed like a branding iron scorching its mark on the earth below. By nine o'clock it was over eighty degrees, with shimmering waves of heat rising from the prairie around the ranch compound to join the dust brought up by thousands of moving cattle.

Jo wiped perspiration from her forehead with her red bandanna and tucked it back into the hip pocket of her jeans as she sat astride her sorrel cow pony and watched the cattle moving slowly south across the north range. In the distance, amid a cloud of brown dust, she could see three of the four other hands on horseback riding at the rear of the herd, their horses taking them on tacking paths to urge straggling cattle along with the others as they made their way at a leisurely pace.

They wanted to move the cattle closer to the ranch, where the grass had not yet been grazed that season and where they would be closer to the main stream rather than relying on the various creeks and rivulets that were beginning to dry up in the late-season heat. They did not, however, want to move the cattle too swiftly. That meant that they were in for a hot and tedious day on the range.

As Jo began riding toward the herd, the sound of Dan's helicopter magnified in the distance. She wheeled her horse around, facing south and scanning the horizon with one hand over her eyes until she spotted the black speck to the southwest. The speck grew rapidly as she sat watching, swelling with its sound until it rushed overhead at about two hundred feet.

The wind of the helicopter rotors flattened the grass around her and blew the brim of her hat down slightly, but her horse didn't flinch at the commotion. Raised amid a variety of vehicles, the animal took the intrusion of this flying beast in stride. For Jo, the brief breeze was a welcome relief from the heat.

Dan wisely wheeled the chopper about before he reached the herd, however, turning to rise almost vertically and hover several hundred feet over Jo's head.

"Hello, boss, over," Dan's voice crackled over the walkie-talkie hanging on the horn of her saddle.

She picked up the radio and keyed the mike switch. "Hey, flyboy, find any loose ones? Over?"

"No, the herd is intact on that end," he replied, his voice made high and crackly by the small speaker in the radio. "Where do you want me? Over."

"North of the herd. Help move them south. Gently, Dan, don't make them run."

"You didn't say over," he came back a moment later.

"Over and out, flyboy," she said, laughing. "We're taking a break at ten. It's sweltering down here."

"Nice and cool up here," he said. "I've got a good breeze going."

"Don't rub it in," she told him. "Go on now. I want to get my money's worth."

"Roger," he said. "Over and out."

The helicopter turned briskly and flew north at the same altitude, not even disturbing the grass in its path. Once he was on the far side of the herd, he dipped lower, flying at reduced speed along the north edge of the mass of cattle, and occasionally dipping toward stragglers as the men on horseback continued to ride herd below him.

Jo noted how the cattle kept up with one another better than they had before. He was able to move over the lagging cattle faster than men on horseback and, as a result, kept them in tighter formation. They were moving a bit faster, however, which wasn't good.

"Hey, flyboy," Jo called into the radio.

"Flyboy here," he answered.

"Don't move them too fast. We're not racing anyone."

"Will do, boss. Out."

He pulled back slightly after that, letting the cattle resume their previous pace by distancing his threatening noise and movement from them.

Jo smiled and nodded in approval. He knew what he was doing, all right, and she needn't worry about her cattle with his noisy bird helping to herd them. But he couldn't do it alone, Jo thought as she set out to head off a small group of adventurous cows who were taking a new tack from the main herd. It still took human beings on horseback to herd cattle.

OVERHEAD, Dan moved the chopper along a zigzag path behind the cattle, trying to maintain enough altitude to avoid adding more dust to the cloud already raised by the movement of the cattle over the broad expanse of land.

The other men had been very clear regarding how they felt about any additional dust he might raise, and he had ensured their camaraderie by obliging them throughout the week. To a man, they were a taciturn bunch. Hank was the most talkative of them, and he didn't say much, either. They were a good crew.

Jay Westall, a lanky, gray-haired fellow of about forty-five, handled the farming for the ranch. He had spent the early-morning gab session rocking back on the hind legs of his chair, chewing on a dead cigar and saying little.

David Burke, the youngest of the group at twenty-five, was blond and bulky, a young bear of a man who sat on the front of his chair as if waiting for an excuse to burst forth in motion.

Bill James, a short, bowlegged wrangler who wore his hat most of the time in an obvious effort to cover his thinning hair, played with a deck of cards while they talked, shuffling and reshuffling for a game that never started.

Hank Driscoll rounded out the quartet. Medium height and thickly muscled, the redheaded cowboy was a commanding presence. He'd held the floor last night with his account of finding the body and his subsequent journey into town to get the sheriff.

"That idiot deputy had been drinking when he showed up," Hank had told the other men. "He went along scuffling his feet through where the killer probably stood. Andrew was pissed but held it in. He's a good man, though a bit too loyal to the likes of Glen Wright."

"I wouldn't trust Glen far enough to throw him," Jay said. "It's not just that he's an idiot, but that he's got an exaggerated sense of his own importance. Men like that shouldn't be given badges."

"Well," Hank said, "he's got one, and he'll probably be out here more than we'd like, so you boys stay on a short rein. Remember, he has a gun to go along with that badge. No trouble. Right?"

"Why would there be trouble?" Dan asked.

"It's too long a story for this time of night," Hank said. "We've got to be out on the range in the morning, while you get to fly around flapping dust in our eyes."

"I'll be careful," Dan said.

"You better," David said, laughing. "There's four of us, remember, and you can't stay in the air forever."

Dan thought of the conversation now, not just because of the remarks about dust but because of the implication of enmity between the ranch hands and Deputy Glen Wright. He wished there'd been more time to talk last night, but there would be plenty of time for that.

Right now he had to concentrate on staying with the herd and watching out for stragglers. Scanning the expanse of land, he saw that they were remaining in a tight group, the cowboys following at an easy pace with occasional movements to urge slower cattle along.

It looked as though they were doing well without him for the moment, so he allowed his path to stray farther toward the western edge of the herd where they were moving along the side of a shallow gully with a dry creek bed at its base. It was pleasant work, and far more interesting than flying a traffic helicopter.

As he began to turn back toward the main herd, a flash of light in the west caught his eye. From this altitude it didn't look as though there was anything there. Still, something had flashed as though the sun had been reflected by a metallic surface, and it would bother him for the rest of the day if he didn't check it out.

Dan aimed his craft toward the memory of the flash and pushed the nose down in an accelerating dive away from the herd. Soon he was skimming about a hundred feet above the ground at full speed, hoping to satisfy his curiosity and get back to work without wasting too much time.

He should have flown higher and much slower to find anything on the ground, of course, but he loved low-level flying and took advantage of any opportunity to engage in it. As it was, he nearly missed his goal, not because he was flying too low to see it, but because he was moving so swiftly that he had passed over it before he was fully aware it was there.

He spun the chopper up and around in a tight loop and hovered at about two hundred feet, looking down at the white cylinder of a tanker truck traveling slowly along a rutted path that ran to the north through the grasslands. The truck bore no markings or company logo, but it was the type of tank that could be used to carry anything from gasoline to milk. After a moment, watching how the sunlight sparkled off the rearview mirror as the truck bounced along the path, Dan headed back to the herd. There was nothing for him to look at there.

Still, why was it driving along a road better suited for four-wheel-drive vehicles? Where on earth could it be going?

He didn't have time to ponder the questions when he got back to the herd, because a group of cattle had broken loose along the west flank just out of sight of the cowboys on horseback. Dan devoted his energies to convincing them to move back in with the others, rather than deal with the noisy monster overhead.

They had made good progress by ten o'clock, when they let the herd slow and then stop to graze in the grass along the stream that ran through the Tate property. The small group of dusty wranglers then dismounted and found comfortable spots to settle down for a moment's rest.

Dan put the helicopter down on a low hill some distance away from the grazing herd to avoid spooking them and ambled down to join the rest of the crew, who were stretching their legs and getting comfortable in the grass near the stream.

There was no shade available to them except that provided by the incline of the hill to the river, and they lay down to take advantage of that slim bit of shelter from the heat of the sun. When the sun reached its zenith, there wouldn't even be that much shade for them, so it was best that they break now and work through the noon hour, breaking again at two. Of course, by that time, they hoped to have the cattle in place on the new grass, so they could return to the ranch.

"How am I doing, boss?" Dan asked as he squatted beside where Jo was lying in the tall grass with her cowboy hat tilted over her eyes.

"You haven't crashed all week," she replied easily. "That's pretty good, isn't it?"

"Not bad." He sat, removing his hat and wiping his forehead with the back of his hand. "It's hot down here."

"Quit lying, now," she laughed, lifting her hat to see him. "You aren't any cooler up there in that Plexiglas oven."

"No, I suppose not." He plucked a stalk of grass from the ground and placed it in his mouth, moving it thoughtfully as he surveyed the countryside. "This is nice," he said after a few minutes. "Very nice. I could do without seeing concrete and steel for a while."

"What kind of flying did you do in the city?"

"Corporate flights. Did some traffic reporting for a radio station, too. Dull stuff."

"I don't know," Jo mused, "maneuvering around a city sounds kind of exciting."

"Yeah, like combat some days." Dan laughed. "But mostly it's just a bunch of air-traffic-control people telling you where and when you can fly, executives telling you where to go and when to pick them up, and deejays telling you to talk faster so they can get to their commercials. And all the while, everything you see is man-made and sterile. It can't be good for a person to live in a box all their life."

"I don't mind the city," she told him. "But I don't know if I could stand to listen to the newscasts every night. Too much crime."

"Well, I guess they don't have a corner on the market," he commented. "Places don't cause things, people do. There's just more people available to cause things in a city, is all. It kind of piles up."

"But I guess it only takes one evil person, doesn't it?"

"That's about the size of it."

Dan sat beside her, allowing his eyes to drift up her body lying relaxed in the tall grass before forcing his gaze to drift once more to the horizon. It was hard to avoid looking at her, even clad as she was in dusty jeans and a checkered shirt. It was very hard, indeed.

"What do you think about our mess, here?" Jo pushed her hat away from her face and lifted herself on her elbows to regard Dan. "I can't think of a reason for anyone to want to kill Pettigrew. Well, want to, maybe, but not to actually do it."

"Had he been in any legal hassles with anyone lately? Any problems besides the cattle?"

"Not that I know of. As you found out over the week, he wasn't the type to keep his complaints to himself. I can't imagine a case where the whole county wouldn't know about it. There hasn't been anything lately."

"What about old grudges? Any unsettled disputes?"

"Not that I know of."

"I suppose that would be tough," he admitted. "Pettigrew might have been public about his complaints, but we're talking about a grudge *against* him not by him. Why was this guy so ornery? It looks as though he had as much as anyone else around here. What was his problem?"

"If he owned everything in sight, it still wouldn't have been enough for Pettigrew," she commented dryly. "Born with a grudge, I guess."

"Was he a newcomer?"

"No, third generation. His family bought into the area about 1900 in a small way and then bought up land during the depression. They bought a few acres from us, too, for that matter. The land just west of here was Tate land originally. There's a sand pit just northwest of us where they got the sand for the concrete in the foundation of the house I'm living in."

"What about the first two generations? Were they easier to get along with?"

"So far as I've ever heard, they got on just fine with everyone. Norton was the troublemaker in the family, but he made enough for all of them." Jo laughed, allowing herself to let some of the worry slip away in their easy conversation. "I remember my parents talking about him. When his father passed on, Norton started overgrazing the land. Made big profits in beef for a couple years before it caught up with him and the herd nearly starved. Had to rent acreage from neighbors to get by until he could sell the beef, and you can imagine that didn't sit well. Everyone in town was full of I told you so's for a while, till they found out how poor a sport he was. I was in grade school then, but I can still remember how he kept everyone up in the air. He made the same mistake a couple years back, too. It seems that he learned his lesson this time, and he came out of it all right."

"Was he an only child, too?"

"No," she said. "His brother was killed in Korea."

"And he never married."

"I think he was engaged once. I don't really know." Jo regarded Dan closely, her eyes narrowed against the sun. "You planning on solving this thing yourself, flyboy?"

"No, I don't have a clue where to start." Dan shrugged, though he might have admitted that she was fairly close to the truth.

If the man hadn't been found on Tate land, he wouldn't have cared one bit about the matter. He had no connection to the crime, after all. But it just didn't look good for Jo the way it was going, and the last thing on earth that Dan wanted was for her to have trouble of any kind. After only a little more than a week, he felt a sense of protectiveness for the woman that he'd never felt for anyone else. He rather liked the feeling.

"I just figure that I should stay up to speed on local events," he explained. "It's my home now, too."

"Is it?" Jo asked. "I mean, do you feel that way?"

"Yes, I do," he admitted carefully. "I like it here, and I certainly like the people."

For a moment, their eyes met, exchanging a feeling that might never have been communicated with words. Maybe there were no words for that feeling, but it was mutual, and the instant their eyes met they knew it. Then they looked away, each knowing that this wasn't the time or the place for the feeling they'd briefly shared. Soon they would have to make the time. That much was certain.

"Did Pettigrew run dairy cattle?" Dan asked, suddenly remembering the tanker truck he'd seen on the late rancher's land.

"No. Not very good dairy land on his spread. Grass is too thin. Why?" Jo was thankful for a new subject of conversation. She didn't trust herself without something to take her mind away from the man at her side.

"I saw a tanker on his land," Dan said. "A white truck. No company logo that I could see."

"Where was that?"

"Just west a couple miles. It was traveling north on a scruffy-looking range road."

"That road doesn't go anywhere but the old quarry that I mentioned," she said, perplexed by the news. "No, I guess it does hit the highway eventually, but there's certainly nothing on it. And it's definitely not a shortcut to anything."

"Driver was probably lost," he said.

"I suppose so." Then a new thought struck Jo, making the matter all the more curious.

"Aren't dairy trucks usually stainless steel?"

"I guess they are. This one was white, though. I guess I assumed it was dairy because it wasn't marked. If it was a chemicals truck, it would have carried the proper hazard markers."

"It's probably nothing, just a new driver who got on the wrong road and couldn't turn around."

"Right."

But, though they'd let it go at that for now, neither one of them was satisfied with the answer. A mysterious truck on Pettigrew land so soon after the murder was just too coincidental, and it seemed as though there had to be a connection.

For the moment, however, the connection eluded them, and they simply sat enjoying the slight breeze that was picking up from the east until it was time for Jo and her crew to mount their horses and Dan to start up his chopper once more to move the herd along.

IN THE TANKER TRUCK, still moving along the rutted road at a measured pace, the significance of the helicopter buzzing overhead hadn't been missed. The driver, a burly red-haired fellow with a tattoo of an eagle on his left forearm, was on the radio as he drove, speaking in short, gruff sentences.

"Came real low overhead," he said into the microphone.

"He's just herding cattle," came the reply, broken by static.

"No way. They're two miles off at least."

"You had better hope he was looking for strays. We're nearly done here and can't afford any other in cidents."

"Take care of him, then," the driver said. "That' why they're paying you so much."

"Yeah, well, you're not the one paying me, are you Shorty? You just get done with your work and leave the rest of it to me."

The driver racked the microphone without further comment, scowling to himself as he continued along the path toward the old quarry. Two more loads and they' be gone without a trace. If he had to kill a pilot to avoid the law, he would do just that. And if that pretty ranch owner gave them any trouble, well, taking care of her would be a pleasure.

Chapter Seven

By the time they had the cattle settled into their new range, the sun was blazing hot with the temperature hovering around ninety. The heat reflecting off the ground was visible as shimmering waves around the riders who returned to the ranch compound at four o'clock. Dan hovered over the riders until they were within sight of the ranch buildings, and then moved ahead to put his craft down gently beside the fuel tank in the yard behind the bunkhouse.

He was checking the fuel tank when the others rode into the compound. David Burke leaped from his horse and sprayed a jet of water over his head from a hose near the horse trough. He gave a satisfied yelp of shock when the cold water struck his hot skin. Then, not satisfied to have just cooled himself off, he turned the hose on Jay Westall, who was walking toward him.

"Cut that out!" Jay yelled, grabbing at the hose. "Geez, Davy, I only want a drink of water, you dumb lunk! Get away from me with that damn thing!"

"Cool off, Jay! Enjoy!" David replied happily as he danced away with the hose in search of his next prey.

"You douse me, you're fired," Jo warned the young hand as he approached her.

He heeded her warning, but caught Bill James instead, chasing him around the edge of the bunkhouse with the hose. Dan was just about to turn the corner when Bill rounded the building, so he hung back a moment until David came by and then grabbed the hose trailing behind him and jerked it back, pulling the young man back onto his rear end and wresting the hose from him.

Putting one finger to his lips to still the young man's laughing protests, Dan took the hose back around the house, gripping the trigger of the spray nozzle firmly as he walked toward Jo.

"Is this what you people do for fun around here?" he asked the unsuspecting woman.

"They're hot, I guess," she replied, mopping her own forehead with her bandanna as she spoke. She almost wished that she had let David spray her for it would have been a welcome relief.

"Now that you mention it, you look a little hot, yourself, Jo," Dan mentioned casually. "You can't be comfortable all dusty and hot like that."

The grin that spread across his face warned her, but Jo only had time for one backward step before he brought the spray nozzle up and squeezed the trigger, dousing his lovely employer with cold water to the great delight of the wet wranglers around her.

"Oooh, you!" she cried out, laughing. Then she called, "Anybody who wants an extra day off this month, grab that chopper jockey!"

Immediately, Dan found himself in the grip of all four of them before he could mount a defense. They carried him, writhing and laughing, by the hands and feet, into the corral and straight over to the horse trough inside.

"Don't get my wallet wet!" Dan begged, laughing. "Come on, guys, have a heart!" But he was deposited into the trough with a loud splash, much to the annoyance of Jo's sorrel who was already at the water. "Ugh!" Dan cried out when he emerged from the water. "This water is filthy!"

"Now that you're in there it is," David agreed. "We should have thought of that, boys. Now we'll have to drain the tank or we'll poison the horses."

Jo's cow pony didn't seem to mind the addition to the tank, however, and dipped her head to drink at Dan's feet while the pilot sputtered and pushed the water from his eyes.

"It's about time you had a proper welcome to Montana, Tex," Jo said. Then she turned to the other men and said, "So, now that we've had our fun, who's on kitchen detail tonight? I'm hungry."

"I am," Jay volunteered. "We're eating at six, so don't any of you varmints be late."

Dan pulled himself from the trough and leaned against the corral fence watching the others walk away. He smiled, beginning to unbutton his wet shirt. These people were all right, he thought, it was a pleasure working with them.

Just wait until he got them up for helicopter rides. That would be a pleasure, indeed.

JAY WESTALL'S CHOICE of chili and corn bread for supper that night seemed a bit intemperate, considering the heat of the day. "Good hot chili is the best thing on a hot day," he explained, dishing up the steaming bowl of beans and beef. "Ain't that right, Tex?"

"Hotter the better," Dan told him. "Though that can't be too hot if the spoon isn't melting."

"The secret to good chili," Jay went on, ignoring the remark, "is that you don't simmer it or do any of that slow-cook junk like people do. No, that just makes the flavors mingle. It takes the surprises out of it. You want to get it together and cook it and be done with it, that's all. Nothing fancy to it at all."

"Yeah, so cut the talk. Just serve it up and be done with it," David called out. "We'll tell you if it's any good, so there's no sense going on about it."

"Whatever you tell me I won't believe, anyway," Jay said, laughing and handing him a bowl. "You've been a darn liar as long as I've known you."

"You boys behave yourselves at the dinner table," Jo said. "You've been good so far, so don't spoil it. I'd hate for Dan to think he's got immature rowdies for range partners."

"I already know that," Dan said. "It's their cooking that I'm still not sure about."

"I can cook," David said, "and Jay's all right. Just don't eat anything Bill makes. He's lethal."

"Hey, one meal!" Bill swallowed quickly to protest. "One bad meal and a guy never hears the end of it. Hell, I still say it would have been all right if you boys hadn't been late getting in. Get off it, boy."

"Yeah, what was that? Something with zucchini? Horrible stuff, Dan, I tell you. Horrible." The young wrangler nudged Dan, grinning. "We had to go into town and eat that night."

"At least you got a night out," Bill said. "We don't normally let you go with us."

"Good chili," Dan commented, ignoring what appeared to be a long-running squabble. "So when does my night come up again?"

"We better wait on that," David said. "Breaking in a new cook is hard work."

"More than you do most days," Jay said.

"Hey, hard work is bad for you," David said. "I don't want to die young from too much work."

"Don't worry, that'll never happen," Bill said. "Maybe you should check into getting a pilot's license, so you can sit in a nice breeze looking down on people all day."

"Nice work if you can get it," Dan said, grinning.

"Wait till we get you on a horse," David said. "We'll get you dusty yet."

"Well, that might take a while," Dan answered. "I don't ride."

"For real?" The young cowboy was amazed by that bit of information. "Jo, you went and hired a hand that can't ride a horse?"

"He didn't say he couldn't ride," she said, doing her best to intercede on Dan's behalf. "He said that he doesn't."

"Same thing," Bill said. He laughed, shaking his head. "You got yourself an urban cowboy here, Jo. Don't you worry, though, we'll break him in."

"I wouldn't try too hard to break him," Jo said. "Not before you ask Ken Zane whether it can be done."

"I think the four of us can get him on a horse," David boasted. "If we sneak up on him, that is."

"Damn you boys talk a lot." Hank spoke up for the first time, shaking his head in resignation. "A body can't hardly digest his food with all this yammering."

"If we're going to be talking, maybe we should talk about something important." Jo looked thoughtfully around the table as she spoke. "You know they'll be around here investigating the murder. Probably it'll be Glen here mostly.''

"Maybe we could arrange a little stampede," Bill suggested. "Nothing fancy, just enough to scare that little pissant off.''

"No, we won't try to scare him off." No matter what she said, the look on Jo's face exposed the fact that she rather liked the idea. "We didn't do anything, so we'll just answer his questions and be done with it. No problems," she added seriously. "Right? No problems?''

"No, ma'am, no problems.''

"What is it with that deputy?" Dan asked. "Is he that bad?''

"He's a runt," Hank said. "A runt with a gun.''

"He needs it to make up for his personal shortcomings," David said, gaining a respectable laugh from his audience.

"Boy, you must own a shotgun then, hey, Davy?" Bill said.

And that was about as serious as the meal-time conversation was allowed to get. Dan's question went unanswered for the time being.

"GLEN WRIGHT LIKES to give people a hard time," Jo explained later as she and Dan sat on the porch watching the sun drop against the vast horizon.

The other men had gone to town, but Dan had begged off, saying he'd rather relax at the ranch. Now he sat on the top step to the porch, wondering what his next step should be. Jo behaved so businesslike in public that it was hard to know whether or not it would be proper to kiss her.

"He's a bully, really," Jo went on, "but he's too small to get physical about it.''

"It sounds more personal than that," Dan commented. "Your crew hates the man."

"He's earned it."

She sipped her iced tea and rocked back on the wooden glider her grandfather had built fifty years earlier. Dan shifted one foot up on the step beside him and extended the other leg out before him. Jo watched him closely, the last glow of the evening sun highlighting his profile in noble relief. She was struck by how easily he had fit into the group on the ranch. He was the type of man who could fit into any situation and look as though he'd been there all along. Intelligent and good-looking, quick on his feet, the man seemed too good to be true. Yet, here he was.

"How did he earn it?" he asked, looking up toward her.

"Come up here so we can hear each other," Jo suggested. She patted the empty space beside her on the cushion. "This swing is built for two, after all."

"I guess it is at that." Dan stood, walked over and sat beside her, the fragrance of her perfume swirled around his head. "And the view is much better over here."

"I'm glad," she replied, accepting the oblique compliment with a shy smile. He made her feel shy, girlish, and she liked the feeling of uncertainty that went with it. It was new to her to feel uncertain about anything, for certainty was something she was born with.

"So what do you think about our little mystery?" he said, trying to keep the conversation on track despite the longing that proximity to this beautiful woman brought about in him.

He didn't want to talk about murder or the deputy. He wanted to talk about her eyes and the soft mystery of her lips. He didn't want to talk at all, but to listen to the music of her voice. He wanted to merely be beside her in silence. He wanted only that, and perhaps she wanted it, as well, but he couldn't quite find the magic that had prompted last night's intimacy. Not when he'd had a day in her company to make him completely aware of what she already meant to him. This resolute woman had been on the verge of allowing an impulsive kiss last night, but he couldn't risk a refusal at this stage of the game. There was too much at stake.

"I don't want to think about it," she replied, echoing his thoughts. "The sheriff will think about it for us."

"I like that idea. What about the deputy?"

"An old feud. Forget it." Jo looked at him closely then, her lips rising into a slight smile. Uncertain or not, she was used to taking positive action and she did so now, letting her words spill out before she could rethink them. "Why didn't you kiss me last night?" she asked.

"Why?" The question caught him off guard. Why? There might be a thousand reasons why, but he suddenly felt stupid explaining them.

"You probably kiss all your bosses," she teased. "I suppose you're sick of it."

"No, I wasn't sure if you would want me to." He smiled then, his wit returning. Dan could feel his heart pounding and wondered why it didn't start the swing rocking to its forceful beat.

"I see," she whispered. She wanted his kiss, his lips on hers and his strong arms around her. If he hadn't figured that much out already, maybe he wasn't as intelligent as she had thought. Or maybe all he needed was some encouragement.

Jo felt herself moving toward him before she was aware of making any decision in the matter. She leaned over, tilting her head, meeting his lips with hers and briefly mingling their desires. Parting, she looked into his eyes and saw the same abandonment of thought and logic that she felt within herself. Then she knew that she was right, and when he moved to return her kiss, she threw her arms around him and fell back against the arm of the glider, heedless of the glass of iced tea that crashed to the floor behind them. Nothing mattered but his kiss, his arms and the explosive need she felt for him.

"I don't believe this is happening," he whispered against her ear, kissing along her jaw to her throat and down toward her heaving chest. "It's a dream, isn't it. Please don't anybody pinch me," he said breathlessly as he continued kissing her, his hot breath enticing her with each word.

"It's no dream," she said softly. His lips pressed hot against her throat and moved up again to find her mouth with his as his broad hands clasped her back, holding her firmly yet gently. She slipped her fingers up through the hair on the back of his head, her hands clutching him with need and hot desire as she returned his kisses with equal fervor.

The pulse of need that had been throbbing within her grew to an incessant roar. This nearness was not enough. Nothing short of consummation would sate her desires now. Nothing short of completion could allow her to keep her sanity in the face of the sudden love that had flown into her life.

But the sound of tires on gravel forced them apart as quickly as if a bomb had exploded between them. Dan released her and stood, backing to sit on the porch rail while she sat up, smoothing her blouse and shaking her hair into place. Both of them affected a nonchalance that they each expected their visitor to see through immediately. Still, they struggled to regain their breath and conceal the heat of passion that still claimed them. Then, as the car pulled up in front of the house, they both began laughing.

"I feel like my parents just drove up," Jo said to him.

"Gee, Mr. Tate," Dan said, affecting a quavering tone, "we weren't up to anything. Honest!"

"Hey, Jo!" Bill James got out of the car and approached the porch quickly. "Jo, David's in jail. You gotta come bail him out!"

Chapter Eight

"What?" Jo's expression darkened as she stood to approach the hand. "What on earth happened?"

"Glen was giving him a hard time," Bill said. "Well, he hit him."

"David did?"

"Yup. Well, he didn't really connect, but he took a good swing at him."

"Oh, hell, do I have to confine you boys to the ranch from now on? What started it?" Jo turned, threw open the door and entered the house with both men following behind her.

"Glen was in the bar with Ken Zane," Bill explained as Jo walked into the office. "Ken was making cracks and David just couldn't keep his mouth shut about it. Glen wouldn't let him hit Ken, and he dressed him down for being drunk and disorderly. Hell, the kid only had two beers. And we all know that David doesn't get disorderly. Three beers just put him to sleep."

"It sounds like he was pretty disorderly tonight." Jo took her checkbook from the desk in the office and returned to the living room. "Where's Hank?"

"At the jail. He wasn't in the bar with us, or he probably would have stopped it."

"You should have stopped it, Bill. Hank shouldn't have to baby-sit." Jo took her hat from the hook near the door. "Now I've got to go see if I can bail the idiot out."

"I know I should've got between them, but I probably would've just decked one of them myself," Bill said as they walked outside. "That Zane fella needs to get knocked down a couple times, Jo."

"Maybe he does, but you don't do it by hitting the deputy."

"What kind of cracks was he making?" Dan asked.

"Oh, he more or less called Jo a murderer, is all. He was looking for a fight."

"And Glen let him talk like that?"

"They're as close as crossed fingers. Of course he let him. He was laughing with him."

"Let's go see if we can get him out." Jo stepped down from the porch and walked toward the car. "Andrew will probably let David out if I put up some kind of bail."

"Let's take the chopper," Dan suggested. "It's faster."

"No way," Jo said. "It's dark out."

"Less likely to hit something on the road up there," Dan said.

"You'd make one hell of an entrance," Bill added.

"You would at that, Jo," Dan agreed.

"Well, it would give the situation a sense of urgency to fly into town, wouldn't it?" Jo found herself smiling despite her misgivings. She rather liked the idea of rushing into town in a helicopter and putting it down right in front of that smug little deputy's feet.

"Okay, I guess I'll survive it," she allowed. "But nothing fancy up there."

"Nothing fancy. I promise."

JO WAS STRUCK by the beauty of the world at night from her vantage point between the earth and sky. The stars overhead seemed brighter, a canopy of sparkling white points of light casting wan illumination on the moving tapestry of shadows that rushed below the helicopter. The ground was blue and black, a blur of humped shadows flowing beautifully, like water, beneath them.

"I'm glad we flew," she said into her microphone.

"I knew it would be rather romantic."

"Oh, you did, did you?" Jo laughed. He was right, in a way, though the noise of the engine was hardly romantic. "It's a beautiful view, anyway."

"Put on the helmet at your feet and look through the goggles," he suggested. "Infrared vision equipment."

"How did you afford all this stuff?"

"It's all used. Surplus. When they upgrade the gear, they practically give the old stuff away."

Jo put the helmet on. It was too large and wobbled badly, but it fit well enough so that she could flip the binocular goggles down and hold them against her eyes. Her view turned remarkable. Suddenly, the ground below them wasn't a blur of shadow, but a sharply defined world colored in green and white. It was as easy to discern the different geographical features as if it were early twilight rather than full night.

"This is great," she said.

"Just one of the many toys they get to play with in the military. We're getting close to town. Where do you want to land it?"

"There's a parking lot across the street from the jail."

"All right, boss," Dan replied. "So where's the jail?"

"Oh, I'm sorry. It's a square brick building just down the street from the bar we were at last night."

"Right. Get ready for final approach."

Jo removed the helmet and watched the small town grow below them. They approached from the northeast, rushing along First Street toward the center of town as they dropped lower until they were skimming mere feet above the telephone wires along the street. Below them, the few people out after midnight got out of their cars or stopped walking to look up at the craft that swept over their heads, their mouths open, their expressions perplexed.

Dan followed the street straight to the heart of town, and then, when Jo pointed out the parking lot, he banked the copter up and around at a precarious angle to hover over the square of asphalt before lowering them to the ground. Glen Wright emerged from the sheriff's office just as they touched the ground and Dan cut the engine.

The deputy was crossing the street, obviously angry, as Dan lifted the canopy and Jo climbed out of the craft.

"I ought to arrest the two of you," Glen began.

"You've got one of my boys in jail," Jo said, brushing past the man and toward the jailhouse as though she were dealing with some annoying bug. "What's it going to cost me?"

"I don't know what kind of bail applies to this, Jo," he protested, hurrying to keep up with her. "He assaulted an officer of the law."

"I don't care what he did. I just want to know how much to get him out." She pulled open the door of the building and walked inside. "Is the sheriff here?"

"Of course not. It's the middle of the night."

Dan had followed behind them, bemused by the sight of the lithe young rancher making the man scamper behind her. She certainly knew how to seize a situation, but he couldn't see how it was going to help her bail the guy out of jail if she antagonized the deputy sheriff at this point.

"Call him, then," Jo commanded. "Or should I call the judge? I'm sure he'd be glad to quote me a price." She slapped her checkbook down on top of the booking desk and waited. "Come on, Glen, let's get this over with."

"Hi, Jo." Hank stood up from the ladder-back chair that he had been balancing back against the wall near the door to the cells. "He hasn't beat the prisoner none that I've seen," Hank said with a smirk. "Of course, I wasn't here the whole time."

"Funny joke," Glen said, scowling at the other man. "I'm not even on duty, Jo, you'll have to ask Gail."

"Where is she?" Jo asked, referring to Gail Winston, one of the other deputies in town.

"She's making her usual rounds past the bars before closing time. She'll be back in a couple minutes."

"Good, then we can talk to someone who can give us an answer," Dan said. He hadn't meant to say anything, but he couldn't resist.

"You," Glen said, eagerly turning toward him after failing to impress Jo with his official capacity. "What on earth are you doing flying that thing in here like that? We've got zoning laws, you know. That ain't an airport out there."

"It's a parking lot, isn't it?" Dan asked. "I'm only parking there."

"For cars. It's a parking lot for cars. I should throw you in a cell, too, you vagrant crop duster."

"Dan is my pilot," Jo said then. "Do you have a problem with where I told him to park?"

"Besides," Dan added, "I'm not a crop duster."

"Oh, you people," Glen said, walking around the desk and opening a book on it. "No," he said, after flipping a few pages. "I don't see any set amount on bail for this offense. Striking an officer is a serious offense."

"He didn't strike you," Hank said.

"Now, Hank, I think I can judge that better than you can."

"Judge, hell, he just didn't hit you. Ask anybody who was there, Glen, and you'll get the same answer. I wouldn't want to go into court with that if I was you."

"False arrest is a serious charge, too," Jo said. "I hope you can make the charge stick when it comes down to it."

"It'll stick," Glen said with assurance. "Don't worry about that. I have a witness to the assault."

"Sure, you've got Ken Zane," Jo snapped. "Any side he's the witness for has got to be the wrong side."

Just then, Gail Winston returned from patrol, pausing inside the door to regard the people before her with wary gray eyes. The trim thirty-six year-old mother of two had been on the force for ten years and had gained a reputation for being the one deputy you could consistently rely on for fair judgment when it came to a public dispute.

"What kind of convention is this?" she asked them as she walked across to her desk where she unstrapped her gun belt and hung it over the back of her chair. "If you're here to bail David out, let's get it over with. I was hoping to catch up on some reading tonight."

"That's what we're here for. Glen doesn't know what the bail is," Jo answered.

"Oh, Glen, you know Andrew's rule," Gail said. "Five hundred bucks a punch is good for altercations."

"But he struck an officer of the—"

"You weren't on duty, Glen," Gail said. "This one goes down as a bar fight. That's all."

"Five hundred," Jo repeated, opening her checkbook. "I think I can handle that."

Five minutes later, the Bar T crew was standing on the sidewalk outside the sheriff's office.

"You get Jay and take David back to the ranch, Hank," Jo said. "And everyone get a good night's sleep. Tomorrow's a working day."

"Yes, boss."

"I'm sorry, Jo," David offered sheepishly. "The two of them were bad-mouthing you, and I—"

"It doesn't matter what they were doing," Jo interrupted, her tone stern. "There's no excuse for throwing the first punch."

"Yes, ma'am."

"All right. Get on home now."

She watched the two wranglers walk away, then turned to Dan, smiling. "Well, that's the end of that," she said.

"Guess so. Do you always have to be their mother as well as their boss?" Dan asked as they began walking toward the chopper. "Must be a lot of work."

"I do feel responsible," she said. "Besides, I can't afford to be shorthanded."

"And what's wrong with that deputy? We never got around to that."

"It's an old feud, really. Nothing much." She paused beside the helicopter, looking back toward the jail. "I just turned down his marriage proposals one too many times, I guess. He's had the Bar T on his list ever since."

"I get the impression that he's got a long list," Dan mused.

"Yes, it's just that we're at the top of it."

DAN STOOD at the bunkhouse window looking at the main house for a long time that night. He watched the house lights wink out one by one, and then remained to watch the darkened building for several minutes. The sixty yards or so that separated him from her seemed like miles, and the interruption David Burke's problem had provided had dropped like a fence between them. Maybe it was for the best, though. Maybe they would have been moving too fast if David hadn't gotten into trouble.

But he didn't believe that. This separation was like a bullet through his heart, each second apart was another drop of his life's blood spilled. He loved her, and that was all there was to it. She already seemed like a part of him.

Then, willing himself to think about something else, Dan wondered about the trouble with the deputy tonight. Something about it bothered him. Had David been set up? From the sound of it, both Glen Wright and Ken Zane had been baiting the young man, goading him into swinging. But why? What would either of them have to gain by trumping up a charge to lock up the young wrangler? He could think of nothing except to get the Bar T crew out of circulation for a while.

"You aren't one of them insomniacs, are you?" Hank said quietly as he stepped into the room through the half-open door. The foreman bunked with David and Bill in the other room, while Dan had chosen the room Jay had occupied with the men who had recently left the ranch. "Better have a shot of whiskey or something," Hank said softly, careful not to disturb the man asleep in the room. "You can't fly if you don't sleep."

"I'm not much for drinking," Dan said. "What do you think about this mess tonight? Was the deputy just being his usual self?"

"As opposed to what?"

"I don't know. Do you think he wanted David to swing at him? From what I heard, it sounds that way."

"I don't think Glen knows what he wants," Hank offered. "He gets ahead of himself sometimes, and then he has to scramble a bit to figure out what he did."

"Was he drunk?"

"No, he hadn't had anything that I saw. Zane was pretty tight, though. Dave probably could've taken him in that condition, but he would've gotten ambushed later for his trouble. Glen probably did him a favor by stepping in the way."

"Maybe." Dan thought a moment about his own run-in with Zane, wondering what kind of ambush he could expect because of it. "But it doesn't seem right."

"Glen is a fool, that's all there is to it."

"What about him and Jo?" Dan knew he probably shouldn't ask, but he felt compelled to know all he could about the situation. "Do you think Glen was using David as an excuse to give Jo grief?"

"Maybe." The foreman's gaze moved over Dan's face slowly as a broad smile spread on his thin lips. "You kind of like the boss, don't you, flyboy?"

"She's a nice woman," Dan said noncommittally.

"Right." Hank laughed. *"Nice."* He clapped Dan on the shoulder, shaking his head in amusement. "Well, you seem like a nice enough fella, so good luck to you, Dan. But I'll warn you, Jo Tate is a mighty particular woman."

"Why? Because she wouldn't marry Glen Wright?"

"Nope, no woman with eyes and ears would ever marry him. Jo just knows what she wants, is all. She wouldn't marry the sheriff when he asked, either."

"She seems to have gathered a few proposals."

"Her share, I expect." Hank's smile faded then, a serious expression replacing it on his weathered face. "She's a special woman. I suspect that most men who know her at all can't ever be satisfied with anyone else after that."

"What about you?" Dan spoke before he thought and wished he hadn't.

"No, I never asked Jo to marry me." Hank smiled then, defusing what might have been a tense situation. "Mostly because I knew she'd turn me down. I reckon that holds true for every man here."

"Besides, you've got a thing for Mary."

"Maybe I do, but that's my business."

"I suppose, but it looked like Mary was baiting you last night," Dan said thoughtfully. "She kept looking over at you while she was going through that act with me. Waiting to get a reaction."

Hank smiled. "Well, she got a reaction, I expect. I gotta confess I saw Kenny come into the bar. Should've warned you."

"I figured that you must have seen him from where you were sitting." Dan smiled. "I understand how it goes."

"It's painful," Hank admitted. "I'd rather be shot."

"Yeah, that about sums it up." Dan looked back at the ranch house, staring at the dark form as though he was trying to see through the walls.

"You've got it bad, don't you?" Hank said, following the younger man's gaze. "Well, that's your business, I guess. Jo's a fine woman, Dan. We'd all do anything for her."

"Would you kill for her?"

"We all would," he said evenly. "Especially Pettigrew."

"So maybe the sheriff actually would have cause to snoop around here?"

"Maybe he would," Hank agreed. "Except that we didn't have a reason to kill him. Being a pain in the ass was just his nature. You don't shoot some dumb cow that won't come out of a gully. You either tease them out or throw a rope around their horns and drag them out."

"Maybe somebody got tired of dragging," Dan suggested.

"Maybe, but it wasn't Jo, and nobody here would get her into trouble by doing something stupid on their own. You got me?"

"I've got you, Hank. And don't worry, I won't be doing anything to get her into trouble, either."

JO LAY IN BED staring at the ceiling and trying to clear her mind of all distractions. She had worked hard that day, and it should have been really easy to fall asleep. But tonight was different, and she couldn't fall into the comfort of sleep as easily as she usually did. Not tonight.

She could readily blame her insomnia on David. The fool had let himself be led into violence by Glen Wright for no good purpose. It was probably a blessing that the boy wasn't a very good fighter. If he had actually struck the deputy, she might not have been able to get him out. It was lucky, too, that Gail Winston didn't like Glen any better than Jo did, or they might have had to wait until morning to bail him out.

Although David was certainly part of her problem tonight, he wasn't the primary reason for her sleeplessness. No, and it wasn't the question of Pettigrew's death, either. It was Dan Fitzpatrick who was keeping her awake and that was all there was to it.

Her lips retained the memory of the pressure of his lips upon them, just as her entire body still seemed warmed by the movement of his arms around her. This saturation of feeling was a new sensation for her, something she'd never experienced in her life. With any man she'd known in the past, there'd always been something missing, some feeling that she knew should be there yet wasn't. It was there with Dan, and she'd known it almost from the first moment.

Now she couldn't sleep because of that feeling, and, pleasant though it was, she needed her sleep. As she had reminded her ranch hands outside the sheriff's office, tomorrow was another workday, and she had work to do.

Work seemed like a poor reason to fall asleep and give up her awareness of this magical feeling. But, if she slept, she might dream of him, and that was an excellent reason to sleep.

She was hot beneath the thin sheet, her satin nightgown sticking uncomfortably to her skin. She decided wryly that August was probably not a good month to fall in love. It was hard enough to sleep on nights like this. She smoothed her hands up over her stomach, pulling at the fabric that stuck there and noticing how rough her hands were.

My God, she thought. *I work like a man and have the hands to prove it.* Though she used lotion regularly, she couldn't ever soothe away the effects of the elements and her grip on the leather reins of her horse. She'd always considered a few calluses a small price to pay for the bounty of her ranch and the freedom of her life on it, but at the moment she wasn't so sure anymore. It wouldn't do to have a man find her unfeminine—not this man, anyway.

She knew, too, that the weather was taking a toll on her face, as well. Too much sun was bad, and she had already had too much of it. Suddenly, every part of her seemed deficient to her, every small scar or callus inflicted by her years of working on the ranch was magnified in her mind until they were all she could see.

Was this what love did to a woman? Did it make her doubt everything about her life? Did she turn into an insecure wreck? Perhaps this was why she'd always shied away from love before. Perhaps she was afraid that it would remind her that she wasn't perfect.

It was too late to avoid love this time. She'd fallen before she was aware of it, and there was no way on earth that she would be able to get up.

Jo AWOKE to the barely audible sounds of movement in the house. She was instantly awake and listening intently, knowing that if it had been one of the hands that had come in, he wouldn't have gone any farther than the refrigerator.

She heard the sound again and then moved swiftly to slip out of bed and into her jeans and a blouse. She stumbled slightly getting into her boots, making a hollow thumping sound on the hardwood floor, which provoked sudden movement beyond her door.

Jo rushed out of her room then, catching a glimpse of someone running through the front door. She hurried in pursuit of the dark figure that rushed across the yard toward the front gate.

"Hey!" Jo shouted. "Stop!"

Moving without thinking, Jo leaped into her Jeep and fumbled the spare key out from beneath the floor mat, starting the vehicle just in time to see the man mounting a horse that was waiting beyond the gate. A light came on in the bunkhouse, but she paid it no heed, throwing the Jeep into gear and wheeling it around to continue her pursuit.

By the time she'd gotten out of the yard, the rider was already headed into the rough territory beyond the fence where an old streambed had cut a deep furrow in the earth. He disappeared below the rise of land, a dark shape swallowed by darkness beneath the moonlit sky.

Jo gunned her Jeep toward him, unable to clearly see the terrain before her as she bounced up to the edge of the hill. She did see that her quarry had had trouble climbing the other side of the gully. He was on foot and struggling to regain his mount, a long dark object in one hand confounding his efforts.

The Jeep shot over the edge of the gully, momentarily airborne before crashing heavily to the ground, the tire catching in loose dirt and tilting to an abrupt halt that spilled Jo out on the ground.

She was dazed for a moment, a burst of stars obscuring her vision. Then she saw the man on horseback again, one arm raised with moonlight catching the gun in his hand.

Chapter Nine

Dan had been lying, fully clothed, atop his bed when he heard Jo's shout from the yard. He had resigned himself to the fact that he wasn't going to be sleeping that night, and so, aside from removing his running shoes, he just hadn't bothered to disrobe.

That decision proved to be a godsend when he heard her calling, and he was up and running from the bunkhouse before she had cleared the yard. Paying no attention to the gravel beneath his feet, Dan ran instinctively to the horses milling around in the corral.

Leaping over the fence, he grabbed the mane of the first horse he came to and swung himself up to its unsaddled back. "Hey, now," he called, kicking his heels against the horse's flank and pulling it around by the mane. "Come on, boy! Hey!" He kicked it into action, and horse and rider circled the corral once, then turned to run at the fence and leap over, landing in stride to follow the Jeep, which had just disappeared beneath the rise of land.

Dan rode instinctively, clutching at the horse with his knees and thinking only of Jo and the fact that her lights had not yet come up from the gully. She must be in trouble!

JO HAD REACTED to the sight of the gun by rolling to her feet and running. But she was winded after her fall from the Jeep and was unable to scramble up the hill toward the ranch. No matter where she might run, she was a very good target in the moonlight, and she could almost feel the weapon being aimed at her back.

Suddenly, she was greeted by the amazing sight of Dan Fitzpatrick bursting over the rise on horseback, reining the steed by the mane as he looked at the vehicle lying on its side below him.

"Dan!" she cried, hurrying toward him. "Dan!"

He urged the horse down the hill toward her, leaning over to the right as he did to reach for her with one hand. His horse bore down on her, and Dan's extended arm captured her under her arms and swung her deftly up behind him even as he urged the animal to greater speed along the bottom of the gully.

A moment later, they were out of danger as the intruder continued on his way to the west and out of sight. Dan brought Jo back to a ranch yard that had come to life in their wake, as the men emerged from the bunkhouse still struggling into their clothing.

"Are you all right, Jo?" Dan asked, holding her shoulders and staring intently into her eyes. "Are you hurt?"

"A bit winded," she said. "I wasn't driving that fast. What about you? That was pretty fancy riding for someone who doesn't ride."

"Hell, Jo," Hank said, laughing. "You never told us he *couldn't* ride. Just that he didn't."

Everyone laughed, their nervousness released in mirth as they gathered around the dusty woman to find out what had happened. Jo couldn't help but notice, though, that Dan was regarding the horse he'd just ridden with a strange look in his eyes. It was as though he'd just awakened from sleepwalking and was amazed by how far he had traveled.

JO EXPERIENCED several moments of disorientation when she awoke that morning. Had she really chased a man from her home? Had Dan really rescued her on horseback? She wasn't sure at first, but the stiffness revealed by her first movements told her that it had, indeed, happened.

Yes, and they had spent an hour going through the house trying to find out if anything was missing—all to no avail. They had been forced to retire without a clue as to what the man had wanted.

The horseman had been carrying something, however. She remembered the long object that had hampered his return to the saddle, but she had no idea what it was. She certainly wasn't missing anything long and narrow like that.

Her first business today would be to call Andrew Hollander about the break-in, but there wouldn't be much for him to do about it. That was why they hadn't called last night—the man was gone and nothing was missing.

The crew would be riding the fence line today, checking for breaks in the wire now that the herd was moving in toward the ranch for the fall roundup. Jo and Dan weren't going out with them, however. There was no work for a helicopter pilot mending fence, after all, and since she was the boss, she could stay home if she wanted to.

Rolling over in bed, her insecurities of last night forgotten, Jo smiled thinking about spending the day alone with Dan. The light streaming in through the window promised another hot, dusty day, but the prospect didn't bother Jo this morning. It was going to be a beautiful day.

David was just finishing putting the men's breakfast dishes into the dishwasher when she entered the kitchen. "Good morning, Jo," he said cheerily. "How are you feeling?"

"Not too bad, considering," she told him. She couldn't help but smile, however, at the young man's unstoppable cheerfulness. She commented on that fact, saying, "You're awfully chipper for a man facing criminal charges."

"I'm just too stupid to be down, I guess," he replied. "Besides, I never laid a glove on him."

"That's not what he said."

"He's lying," David said simply. "Not that I don't wish I had hit him."

"What happened?" Jo took the pitcher of orange juice out of the refrigerator, poured herself a glass and sat at the table with it. "Why on earth did you go off half-cocked like that?"

"That Ken Zane," the wrangler replied, drying his hands. "He was going on about Pettigrew and all. When he saw me, he started talking about how you probably had one of us kill him because of the cattle. He said you were...well, he wasn't nice, is all. Besides, your night was more exciting than mine, anyway."

"Maybe, but we're talking about your night, not mine," Jo said, sticking to the subject. "So, Zane wasn't nice? And you decided to get into a fight with him. Because he wasn't nice?"

"Well, I got riled."

"What did he say, David? You're not the type to pick fights. I'd like to know what got you so angry."

"It was nothing, I guess," he said, clearly embarrassed. "Maybe I was drunk."

"Hank said you weren't. What was it that Zane said?"

"He...well, he said you were probably having... you know...having your period and it got you all cranky. He said that was why you had one of us kill Pettigrew for you."

"And Glen let him talk like that?" Jo spoke calmly, showing no sign of the anger that was boiling inside of her. If Ken Zane had said that to her face, she'd have struck him, too.

"He didn't object," David said. "He seemed to be having a pretty good time."

"I imagine that he was. Well, I thank you for your gallantry, David, but you'd be better off counting to ten next time."

"I'll do that," he said. "At least, I'll try."

"All a man can do is try," Jo allowed. "Now you'd better catch up with the others. I'm going to stay here and do some paperwork."

"Right." He slapped his hat onto his head and threw open the back door. "Looks like we've got another late riser on our hands," he said as he stepped out. "'Morning, flyboy. Or maybe I should say cowboy. Pretty fancy riding, for a city slicker, Dan."

"Good morning," Dan said, passing the man on his way out. "Good morning, boss."

"Good morning." Jo smiled brightly as he walked into the kitchen and stood rather uncertainly before her. "We both missed breakfast. I'll whip something up for us."

"I can help," he offered. "How are you?"

"I'm fine," she said casually. "A bit stiff. A couple bruises. That's all."

"You sure?" He placed one hand carefully on her shoulder and examined her face with a serious, probing stare.

"Yes, I'm sure. I just wish I knew what he wanted with me."

"Could have just been a thief," Dan proposed.

"I doubt that. A thief would have better luck in daylight when we're all out on the range."

"Did you call the sheriff?"

"Yes. He wasn't in, but I gave them a quick rundown, and I'm sure he'll get back to me."

"That's taken care of for now then. I wasn't too sure what I'd be doing today. Hank said they'd be mending fences."

"You can take an overhead tour later to check the herd. Just relax now. You've only been here a little over a week. You don't have to do everything all at once."

"No wonder you feel compelled to act like a mother if you baby your new arrivals like this." Dan laughed, shaking his head happily.

"Well, maybe not all the new arrivals. Just my heroes on horseback." Jo felt herself blushing and quickly turned away from him. This was all so strange to her that she didn't know how to behave. "David was right about your riding. Going over the corral fence and scooping me up like that on bareback is pretty fancy. It takes a bit of training. Where did you learn to ride?"

"Dallas horse club," he said. "Junior rodeo, that type of stuff."

"Really?" She looked at him again, shaking her head. "Yet you don't ride. What's the deal?"

"Horse threw me, and I never got back on," he said, shrugging. "It's been so damn long since I rode, I didn't think I could still do it."

"Now you know that you can."

"Thing is, I don't know if I could again. Not without strong provocation." He spoke thoughtfully and with complete seriousness, honestly unsure of his ability to ride again.

"I'm sure the boys will get you on a horse again one way or another," she said, smiling. "Scrambled eggs all right? You're not one of those low-cholesterol types, are you?"

"No. Whatever you like." He walked up behind her, reaching to grasp her shoulder but stopping himself abruptly. "Jo, about last night, I—"

"Are you sorry you rescued me?"

"No, I meant earlier."

"Oh, you're sorry you kissed me."

"No, not at all. In fact, if I remember it correctly, you kissed me first."

"Yes, I suppose I did. Does that bother you?" Jo spoke quickly, feeling insecure again. She kept her face turned away, afraid to see any doubt in his green eyes.

"No. But, I—"

"But you're afraid that I got the wrong idea about you? That you don't really feel . . . well, the same way about me that I seem to feel about you?" she said.

"No, I . . . oh, here, this is what I mean."

Dan grasped her shoulder and turned her to him, his arms slipping around her as he moved confidently to capture her lips with his. He kissed her firmly, his tongue lingering at the edge of the kiss as one arm held her to him and the other hand slipped down over her jeans to cup her bottom softly. When he broke the kiss, he only parted far enough to gaze passionately into her eyes.

"You're not much of a mind reader, are you?" he whispered. "I'll give you one more chance. What am I thinking now?"

"Let me think." Jo paused, trying to capture the breath that seemed to be flowing out of her rather than in. She felt dizzy, as though she might explode, and the proximity of their bodies betrayed a similar feeling in the man who held her. "If I'm right, you're thinking that you'd rather wait on breakfast for a bit. An hour, maybe."

"Well, maybe you're not so bad at reading minds, after all. I think I'm reading that you agree with me," he said. "Am I right?"

"Yes," she said, sighing. "Yes, you are completely right."

They kissed again, her hands slipping over his tanned face, holding him as though making sure the man who held her was real. Then she allowed her hands to wander as his were wandering, savoring his firmly muscled body and anticipating a fuller knowledge. She'd never known the giddy upheaval she was feeling right now, never had reason to feel her heart pounding in her chest like this. She was light-headed, numbed everywhere except for the places where they were in contact—and those parts were acutely aware of the physical sensation of their bodies pressing together. It was as though the nerves in the rest of her body had given up their ability to feel in order for a few select nerve endings to be especially aware.

His hand slipped beneath the waistband of her jeans in back, hot fingers spreading a tingling warmth to her very core, as his lips inflamed her throat and warmed he flesh within the vee of her cotton blouse. She was ugging at his shirt before she knew it, pulling it free of is jeans to slip her hands over his smooth flesh as she issed his forehead and his rising face, kissed his lips nd the prickly stubble on his throat.

They moved in tandem, finding the buttons on each ther's shirts as they made staggering progress out of he kitchen into the living room. Jo stopped then, ushing regretfully back to remove the boots, which had tubbornly refused to be toed off. She nearly fell in her ffort before Dan caught her and knelt to remove the ther boot. And then he rose, parting her blouse to let t fall as he thumbed open the clasp of her bra between er heaving breasts.

Jo let that garment fall, too, standing in shivering nticipation as he carefully touched her and then leaned o kiss her chest just below her collarbone. When he fted his face, she could see that there wasn't even a limmer of doubt in his soulful green eyes.

"Damned if I don't love you," he whispered, and he ounded amazed by the thought of love, saying it again s if to make certain it was he who uttered the declara- ion, "I love you."

"I love you," she answered, equally amazed.

Dan lifted her in his arms, carrying her toward the all leading away from the living room as she buried her ace against his shoulder and kissed the hot skin that ad been exposed when she opened his shirt. There was othing missing from her feelings about this man. No, e was complete, and she was complete with him.

The world at large seemed far away just then, a hadow play beyond the real world that existed only ere in her home with this man. The only reality in this orld was the touch of his lips on her breasts, and the warm pressure of his hand sliding down her body. But reality has ways of intruding on any private world, and the telephone made its intrusion just as the eager lovers entered the bedroom.

"No," Jo cried as they fell to the bed together and rolled, kissing, dreading the thought of answering the incessantly ringing telephone. "One more ring and they'll give up," she said breathlessly. "Please, God, make them hang up."

"They're not hanging up," Dan said after two more rings. "It's probably that damn sheriff. Don't you have an answering machine?"

"Yes." She kissed his chest, caressing him as she fought with the stubborn buckle of his belt. "But it's not on. I never have it on when I'm at home."

"So that means that whoever is calling probably knows you're at home," Dan reasoned.

"I'm afraid so."

"You'll have to rethink that strategy."

"Definitely." Another ring. "It's not stopping. I better answer it."

Dan let her roll to the phone, watching her pick up the receiver with rapt attention to every movement of her slim form. She was so beautiful, and he couldn't believe that he was here with her. A woman this perfect couldn't possibly have any use for a man like him—yet here he was with her. But even as he watched her and thought about the strange hand fortune had dealt in putting them together like this, he saw her expression darken and the purpose of their morning together change drastically.

"I hadn't expected you to find out so soon, Doc," she was saying, holding the receiver tightly in one hand. "You're sure about this?"

And his reply didn't sit well, for she balled up her other hand and snapped it down atop her thigh in exasperation. Then she cradled the receiver against her shoulder and stood to zip her jeans and rebuckle her belt.

"Okay, I'll be ready for them," she said. "No, we didn't do anything with the carcasses, Doc. You're really sure about this?" Taking the receiver back into her hand, she looked around for her blouse before remembering where they'd left it, and then she smiled in resignation at Dan. "All right, thank you." Jo hung up the phone.

"Bad news?"

"Very bad. I'm sorry, Dan." She knelt on the bed again, leaning to kiss him lightly, then again with greater fervor. "I really hate to have this happen just now. I mean, I really hate to have this happen."

"We've got time," he said. "I'm not going anywhere."

"You mean that?" Taking his face in both of her hands, she gazed deeply into his eyes. "You're not going to get into that bird of yours and fly away some day?"

"Never," he promised. "Not as long as you give us a place to roost, I won't."

"Then you won't." She kissed him again just to seal the memory of his lips on hers. Then she backed away from the bed, feeling deliciously naughty standing before him half-dressed in broad daylight. She saw nothing but adoration in his eyes when he looked at her, and her final misgivings evaporated like morning dew.

"So," Dan said, standing beside her. "What about the cattle?"

"Chemicals." They walked to the living room together, reassembling their clothing. "The cattle were
poisoned with some kind of chemical with a nasty, long
name that shouldn't be out here at all. A residue from
coal-shale refining, he says. Must have been dumped
out here someplace."

"Chemical dumping?"

"Yes, and we're in the center of it."

"They don't figure it was on your land?"

"Doc doesn't figure anything at all, but that doesn't
matter. Until we know what was dumped and where, we
won't be moving any cattle off this land."

"What's the first step?"

"An animal removal service is on its way out to pick
up the carcasses right now. I've got to meet them and
show them where to go. The sheriff will be out later,
too."

"What should I do?"

"Ride the herd," she told him. "Move them farther
onto our land and away from Pettigrew's property. The
boys are working on the fence on the east range, just
drive them easy along the river toward the fence line."

"I'd rather stay with you, Jo," he protested.

"And I'd rather keep my herd safe. Just don't run
them too fast, Dan." She slipped her arms around him
and raised her face to accept his lips on hers. "That's
the best thing you could do for me, Dan. Just get my
cattle away from Pettigrew's land, because you know
that if there is any chemical dumping going on around
here, that's where it is."

"That tanker truck I saw yesterday?"

"It seems likely, doesn't it? And I'd guess that card
in Pettigrew's wallet was there for a reason, too. Well,

I've got to get going. Now that we've missed breakfast, we'll just have to meet for lunch.''

''It's a date.''

He walked with her to the front porch and watched her climb behind the wheel of her dented Jeep, which Hank had pulled from the gully and parked by the corral. When she had slipped the vehicle into gear and roared out of the ranch yard, he walked purposefully to the bunkhouse and entered his room. He had spread the wet contents of his pockets out on the dresser and the windowsill to dry the previous afternoon. Now he retrieved his flight notebook, the pages crinkled and stiff from his dunking in the horse trough. Some of them stuck together, but the page where he'd copied down the numbers from Norton Pettigrew's wallet were loose and the ink hadn't run. He tore that page out and slipped it into the breast pocket of his shirt, snapping the flap closed over it.

He left the rest of the things where they lay and hurried out to his helicopter. There was work to be done, and he had to get to it right away. But he didn't think the most important item was the cattle just yet. No, the first thing he wanted to do was to get a look at the old quarry Jo had said was at the end of the road where he'd seen the truck.

He would herd cattle after he'd visited what he suspected was the scene of the crime.

Chapter Ten

Jo could see the dust raised by the approaching animal recovery vehicles in the distance as she was driving out to where they'd found the first cattle. They were approaching fast as though some special urgency propelled them.

There was great urgency in the task, of course. The cattle had died from the effects of ingesting a poisonous chemical compound that was most often found in oil shale operations. The only way for the chemicals to have gotten into the cattle was for someone to have trucked it up here and dumped it onto the range land.

Montana produced a fair amount of lignite coal and much of it was processed to produce a low-grade oil that was then further refined into other oil products. But there was no mining near the Bar T Ranch, let alone oil refining, so it could not possibly be argued that the chemical had gotten there either naturally or accidentally.

The cattle had been found on her land, which meant that she would be the first person to come under suspicion in the matter. The fact that the investigation would eventually include Pettigrew land was no consolation, for an investigation of this type might take months. And, because of the seriousness of the poison involved, she wouldn't be able to ship any of her cattle to market until the source of the contamination was found and contained. Even though she was sure she would eventually be proven innocent, the effects of the matter would be devastating in a business where this year's profits are essential for next year's operation.

The worst part was probably the fact that there was federal land involved in the case, as well. The Tate and Pettigrew ranches were bordered at the north by federal grazing land on which they both leased grazing rights. It was all too possible that the cattle got poisoned on that land before dying on her land. That meant that it wouldn't be just the EPA investigating, but the FBI, as well.

Jo felt a sour certainty as she drove that things were going to get a lot darker before the next dawn. There was a distinct possibility that she would face bankruptcy before all was said and done.

She could even lose the ranch if the investigation took too long.

THE HELICOPTER SKIMMED over the rolling rangeland, fifty feet above the grass and brush that blurred beneath its speeding shadow and the pressure of the whirling blades. Dan had made one quick pass at the western edge of the herd, urging them to start eastward, and then set himself on this course to the west and north. Now he passed the unmarked border between Tate and Pettigrew land—a demarcation that no one but the ranchers themselves could see—and rushed on to the rutted road leading north.

Over the road, he wheeled the chopper tightly north, a military turn executed with military precision and de-

signed to present the least opportunity for enemy fire to
find the craft. He kept to this low flight path not out of
military necessity but out of a desire to make his journey without being seen. There was a lot of horizon in
Montana, and the higher he went, the more likely he
was to be spotted.

The road below him made a straight track in the
ground, except to navigate around a couple low hills,
and led him to a broad scar in the side of a hill where
sand had been excavated. There was no sign of life in
the gravel pit now, though there were signs of trucks
having recently used the place.

Dan lifted his bird up in order to get a more complete look at the site. From a higher elevation, the
seemingly inconsequential shadows and ridges resolved
themselves into clearly visible tracks of heavy trucks. He
could see the patterns where they'd driven in and
backed around again, apparently backing up to the edge
of a darkened spot in the pit. That would be where they
dumped it.

Dan took his craft down, lowering himself quickly to
land in the center of the brown scar in the dull green
grassland. Then he climbed out and walked to the dis-
colored depression where he'd seen the tracks leading.

There was definitely an oily smell here, though it was
faint and varied with the movement of the slight breeze
in the hot morning air. The discoloration in the sand
was barely visible down here, but Dan knelt at the edge
of it and took a pinch of sand between his fingers, rolling the grains away until there was nothing but a greasy
residue between his fingers. Something had been
dumped here, that was certain.

Dan stood and started back toward the helicopter,
thinking of getting an envelope or something to take a

sample of the sand with him. His plans were changed quickly, however, when he saw three riders approaching from beyond the narrow road.

"So much for your life as a spy," he said grimly. Then, considering the situation, he decided it might be best to get away before he was forced to answer any questions. It was obvious from the speed at which they were riding that they'd already seen him, so there was no point in laying low.

He sprinted to the chopper, climbed in and revved the idling engine, bucking into flight and swiftly rising straight up until the horsemen were mere specks below him. Then he headed east again, making his way back to the herd and his task of moving them toward the other side of the ranch and away from the dangers of the soil contamination.

It smelled like oil, he thought as he flew. *But I didn't notice any oily smell on the cattle. You'd think if they were walking through grass contaminated with it, they would have carried some of it off on their legs.*

But they hadn't, and that bothered him. Something had obviously been dumped in that pit, but was it the same thing they were looking for? It could be that some trucker had just dumped some old crankcase oil in the sand. That in itself was illegal, of course, but not on par with dumping the stuff that had killed the cattle. Without tests, there was no way to be certain.

What he wanted to do now was to move the cattle along a respectable distance and then get to a telephone where he could try out the numbers they'd gotten from Pettigrew's wallet. Jo might want to know of his progress so far, though, so he keyed on his radio and took the mike in hand.

"Flyboy to Jo," he called out over the sound of his engine as he flew in slow loops over the western edge of the herd. "Do you read me? Over."

A minute passed and he called her again before she came on the line.

"Jo here. What's up?"

"Cattle are moving fine," he said first, letting her know he was on the job despite his brief detour. "I took a look at that gravel pit, Jo. There's oil in it."

"What's that?"

"Some kind of oil dumped in that sand pit," he repeated. "I don't know what, exactly. Plenty of tire tracks, too."

"What were you doing there?" She didn't sound displeased, though she did convey the impression that she might have liked to have known about his mission before he undertook it.

"Thought I'd take a look. There were three men on horseback who saw me leave," he admitted. "You might be getting a call from someone."

"All right. I'll keep that in mind. Meet me at the ranch for lunch."

"Right, Jo. Over and out."

"Jo out."

Dan returned his full attention to the herd, gently using the noise and wind of his steel bird to move them along the ground like a brown sea amid the dusty grass below.

And, as Dan continued his work, a man in a battered pickup switched off his radio receiver and sat tapping one stubby finger on the dashboard of his vehicle. It was too late to cover for the oil in the sand pit now, but they could still throw suspicion back Jo's way if they acted quickly.

The government would have investigators on their way soon, so it was time he made sure they would be able to find something on Tate land. He would take care of that tonight.

"THE HERD is nearly at the fence line," Dan said, sitting at the kitchen table with the sandwich he'd just constructed from cold cuts and lettuce. "They're well away from Pettigrew land."

"What about that sand pit?" Jo looked across at him in concern. "And why did you decide to go there?"

"Just a hunch. It didn't seem like anything more than oil, though. And I don't imagine the cattle would have grazed in there, anyway."

"No. Doc Hollander said the stuff would have killed them pretty quickly, too. It's a long walk from there to where we found them."

"So the dump site must be closer to the boundary between your land."

"I would think so." Jo took a bite of her sandwich, chewing thoughtfully for a moment. "I don't know if I should even mention Pettigrew land when the federal people get here. They have a way of reversing their logic to suspect anyone who volunteers information."

"You're right there," Dan admitted. "Can you afford a long investigation?"

"No. I've got to get this herd in to market on time to keep my loans current. I suppose there's enough in the bank to cover us, but not if we have to feed a herd of this size all winter," she explained. "And we'd be sunk in the spring."

"If the stuff is that toxic, there's no way a contaminated cow could live long enough to get to market. That's just simple logic."

"Of course. But this is a government investigation we're talking about, Dan. Not a logical one. Besides, there's no telling what else might have been dumped," she admitted. "And I'd hate to ship bad beef."

"Then I suppose we can't wait for them to follow their own course. We'd better do something to cover our own rear ends."

"I suppose you're thinking of making some phone calls," Jo said, nodding. "That's probably the next logical step."

"We're on the same frequency there, Jo. The sheriff has probably already made the call, but that doesn't mean anything will come of it."

"Right. Do you have the numbers?"

"Here they are." He took the slip of paper from his pocket and laid it on the table between them. "We already know the top one is for that chemical hauler. We should probably try one of the others first. So who makes the call? You or me?"

"I'd better. I can always pretend I'm somebody's secretary if they get nosy." She took the paper and walked over to the telephone, lifting the receiver as she studied the numbers on the sheet. Then she dialed the New Jersey phone number and waited while the phone rang on the other end.

"Hello," an efficient woman's voice came on the line.

"Hi. To whom am I speaking, please?" Jo asked.

"This is Mr. James's office," the woman said. "I'm his secretary."

"Oh, I'm sorry," Jo said quickly. "I must have dialed the second number here. I was trying to get your main office. This is James Chemicals, isn't it?"

"Yes, but this is Mr. James's private line."

"Well, maybe you can help me. I am inquiring about your disposal service," Jo said. "Do you cover the entire United States?"

"No, we're only licensed to handle the tri-state area," the woman said. "Where are you calling from? Perhaps I could recommend a hauler."

"No...well, maybe you could at that," Jo answered. "I'm calling from Montana. A fellow here gave me your numbers, but he's new in the area and I guess he didn't know you weren't nationwide."

"Probably not," she said. Then after a moment, she added, "Here, I think that Great Sky Hauling can help you. Do you have a pad and paper?"

"Just a minute." Jo grabbed a pen from the cup near the phone and used it to take the number down on the paper Dan had given her. "Yes, I've got that," she said. "Thank you very much. Bye now."

"Well?" Dan asked when she returned to the table.

"It was James Chemical," she said. "The owner's private number."

"Great! What did you find out?"

"They don't do anything out here, but the secretary gave me the number for a company called Great Sky Hauling."

"Are you going to call them?"

"Yes, I reckon I will," she said thoughtfully. "I can't help but think that the name of that company sounds familiar, though."

"I suppose a lot of companies up here use the words *Great Sky,* or *Big Sky,* or some other form of that in their names."

"Yes, I imagine so. Well, I suppose I can give them—"

But she was cut off by the opening of the kitchen door as Hank came through, removing his hat and pushing his damp hair back from his forehead.

"Why are you pushing those cows our way?" he asked, opening the refrigerator. "We've really got to hustle to tighten up the wire and keep them off the national parkland."

"Sorry, Hank, I should have given you boys a call," Jo stated as the man brought a glass of lemonade to the table. "Doc Hollander called with the lab results this morning, though, and I thought we'd better get the herd away from Pettigrew land."

"What's the bad news?" the man asked sourly.

"I can't remember the name of the stuff, but they found a toxic residue in the cows. Something from coal-shale refining," she told him. "It looks like someone has been dumping chemicals on the range."

"Pettigrew," Hank said. "That shortsighted bastard would allow anything for a quick buck."

"That's what I figured," Jo said. "He probably made a money deal to get out of the hole during the recession. I knew he got caught, but I just figured that he'd worked his way out on his own."

"He might not have known about it," Dan said, playing devil's advocate for a moment. "They could have easily hauled it in at night and dumped the load."

"No, if someone was making money doing something illegal, you can be sure Pettigrew was in on it," Hank insisted. "You didn't know him, Dan."

"Yes, but he might have been killed because he found out."

"He probably asked for a larger cut," Jo said.

"Always was greedy," Hank added.

"Okay, so we'll say he was in on it. Why would he poison his own land?"

"Money." Jo took her plate to the sink and rinsed it off. "He was a speculator all his life, Dan. I suspect that he came up short a time or two and needed the cash. I might be able to get a line on his stock transactions, though I'd have to call in a few favors. There might be a clue there."

"Why are you bothering with that?" Hank put his glass down empty. "The sheriff will handle it."

"All in due time he will," Jo said. "We've got to try to come out ahead of them on this, Hank. I can't afford a long investigation, and the government might impound the herd all winter if they don't come up with definite answers."

"Good point. Which is why you want the herd on the other side of the ranch."

"Exactly," Dan said. "But you're only what, twenty miles or so from the other ranch down here? Shouldn't we run them farther north around the top of that national parkland? You could get farther from the contamination up there, couldn't you?"

"The grass is worn-out up there," Jo said. "That's mostly federal land north of us. There isn't as much water to keep the grass all summer. We've got to keep them down here where the grass is fresh."

"What about selling the herd off now?"

"We'd take a big cut in profit if we did," Jo said. "We'd have to sell them to a feedlot. A large percentage of our profit comes from selling range-fed cattle. People don't like the antibiotics they use in feedlots. Besides, I don't want to sell the herd unless we know they're uncontaminated. I'd rather go bankrupt than sell bad beef."

"From the sound of it, any cows that got into that stuff are dead," Hank said. "Hell, if they're still standing, they're fine."

"That's what we figure, too. But we can't be sure. We've just got to make sure that the investigation comes to a real quick conclusion."

"Okay," Dan said. "So what's our next move? Do we call Great Sky Hauling?"

"Great Sky?" Hank asked. "Isn't that one of the outfits Ken Zane sells for?"

"Yes!" Jo exclaimed. "That's why it sounded familiar. Zane is connected to them in some way."

"From what I saw, just hiring Zane makes them guilty of something," Dan offered. "What's his connection?"

"He's a feed and grain salesman, but he handles a bunch of different companies in one way or another," Jo said. "You don't see him selling much, though, mostly just hanging around town. But he does do quite a bit of business with Pettigrew's ranch."

"So maybe we don't want to call them," Dan said. "Let's just assume they're dirty and Zane is the local connection."

"Good plan," Hank said. "But what is it about them, anyway?"

Jo and Dan filled him in on what they had so far, admitting to their search of Norton Pettigrew's wallet the other night. The foreman listened with a sour smile on his face, rubbing the stubble on his jaw thoughtfully.

"I guess you don't want to tell the sheriff about the phone numbers then, do you?" he said.

"No, but he'll be following that lead, anyway," Jo said.

"Of course, he'll be saying that he's the sheriff," Dan said. "All they would tell him was that they didn't handle anybody out here and that would be that. I don't suppose they'll volunteer information about Great Sky."

"Right," Jo said. "Though I think we'll still hold off on telling Andrew anything just yet."

Just then, the wail of a siren cut off any further conversation, and the three of them hurried out through the living room to the front porch in time to see two sheriff's cars and two unmarked cars pulling into the yard.

"You and the boys mind the herd, Hank," Jo said quickly as the men got out of the cars. "Ask around about Ken Zane if you can, but don't be too obvious. All right?"

"Right." Hank put his hat on and stepped off the porch, passing Andrew Hollander without a word.

"'Afternoon, Jo," the sheriff said. He didn't look the least bit happy, though Glen Wright was smiling behind him. "I've got a warrant to search the ranch. I'm officially serving it to you right now."

"Search away, Andrew," Jo told him as she stepped down to accept the folded paper he held out to her. She didn't bother looking at it, but continued to smile at the officer. "Did you add some deputies?"

"These are federal investigators, Jo," he explained. "The Environmental Protection Agency will have a crew out soon, too. The FBI is involved because there's a chance that chemicals were dumped on federal land."

"I suspect so, Andrew. I know nothing was dumped on my land."

"That's good, Jo, very good. And even if there was some, I wouldn't imagine that you knew about it."

"So what are you searching for here?"

"Evidence concerning chemical dumping and how it might relate to the death of Norton Pettigrew." A balding man in a gray suit and sunglasses stepped up to the sheriff's side, speaking in an authoritative manner. "We expect your complete cooperation in the matter, Miss Tate."

"You've got it." Jo turned to Dan then, saying, "It looks like I'm going to be tied up here, Dan. Could you take care of moving the herd by yourself?"

"Of course, boss," he said. He took his own sunglasses from his shirt pocket and put them on as he turned to look at the federal agent. "I don't suppose anybody cares that this woman's home was broken into last night," he said. "Or that she was nearly killed chasing the man away."

"We're checking into that, too," Andrew said as Dan stepped down from the porch. "I had a complaint about you, Dan. Don't go flying over Pettigrew land anymore."

"Why? Do they have title to the airspace overhead?" Dan couldn't stop himself from talking no matter how much better it might have been to curb his tongue. Freedom of the skies was always important to him, and he didn't like artificial restrictions.

"No, but the way things are, it just looks suspicious having anyone from the Tate ranch flying over Pettigrew land."

"I'm not equipped to dump chemicals on their property, Sheriff. They don't have to worry about that. Of course, if they're worried that I might see something, that's a different matter."

"Just stay back, okay? And don't land it in town anymore, either. I don't need this aggravation."

"I'll try, Sheriff." Dan smiled and began to walk away, but the FBI agent stopped him.

"Is that helicopter yours, son?" he asked.

"Yes, all paid up."

"That's a military aircraft. You can't fly that without the proper paperwork. Are your papers in order?"

"Yup," he said solidly.

"Better be, or we'll have to impound it."

"You'd better have an airtight warrant before you try," Dan said. "I can be out of your jurisdiction pretty fast."

"Federal jurisdiction is pretty broad ground," the man said.

"What's your name? I didn't catch it."

"Special Agent James Harden," he said.

"Well, Jimmy, you come check my paperwork anytime you like. I've got work to do at the moment." He walked away from the man and past the other agents waiting by the cars.

"Nice bird," one of them said, nodding.

"You fly?" Dan asked him, stopping in surprise.

"Army," he replied, smiling. "Just ferry investigators around now."

"Maybe you can take her up for a spin sometime," Dan said.

"I'd like that," the man said.

"Grimes!" Agent Harden cut off their conversation. "This isn't a social club here. Have your army reunion later."

"Later," the man told Dan, shrugging.

Dan walked back to his helicopter and started the engine. He took a moment to make sure that he did, indeed, have the necessary papers in his flight case and then took off toward the herd. Everything was in order, so there was nothing to worry about. Still, if the feds did try to give him trouble, he had a few relatives he could call as a last resort. His family hadn't been in Texas politics for a hundred years for nothing, and there's no point in having an uncle in Congress if you can't get a favor out of him every once in a while.

Jo LED THE MEN into the house thinking about the exchange between Dan and Agent Harden. He had reacted like a typical Westerner to the intrusion of authority. In fact, his reaction, illogical and confrontational as it might be, was exactly how her father would have responded had someone threatened to impound his property. Her own gut reaction was about the same, though in this case there could be no denying them access to her office.

"We'll want to go through all your papers and computer records for the past two years, Miss Tate," Agent Harden said once they had all filed into her small office. "My men are trained accountants, and they'll need to use this room for their work. If you have any checkbooks or other items necessary for current operations, I'm going to ask you to remove them now. We can't allow you to come back in here until we're finished."

"My own office?" She felt her own stubbornness rising then, her temperature rising with it. "You're locking me out of my own office?"

"Yes, until we're finished with the investigation, we are," he replied. He took his sunglasses off, revealing a set of dark, wide-set eyes. "We can't risk your tampering with evidence."

"And how long do you expect it to take?"

"No more than a week," he said.

"A week?" Jo looked to Andrew in appeal. "Have you got a crew out at Pettigrew's, too?"

"No, we don't," he admitted, scowling. "The ranch is going into probate, and a group of accountants is out there already. We'll use their data."

"But it's one hell of a lot more likely that Pettigrew was the one allowing chemical dumping," she said. "You should get to work on that."

"We don't have any evidence against Pettigrew at the moment," the federal agent said. "If evidence is obtained, we will certainly investigate the possibility."

"And you've got evidence against me?" she asked him.

"Circumstantial, yes."

"What? Andrew, are you people honestly accusing me of illegally dumping chemicals on my own property? That's insane!"

"No, we're not," Andrew assured her uncomfortably. "I know you wouldn't knowingly poison the land, Jo."

"So what kind of evidence has he got?"

"Just circumstantial, like he said," the sheriff replied. "Hell, Jo, I might as well tell you that it's the murder we've got something on."

"Which provides circumstantial linkage to our dumping problem," the agent elaborated. "Now, if you have anything to take out of here, please do it now."

"But what have you got?" She barely heard Harlen's words after Andrew had spoken. Murder? They had evidence against her? "What have you got that makes you think I killed Norton Pettigrew?"

"Jo, I can't tell you that." Andrew frowned, obviously distressed at his position in the matter. "I'm not pressing charges at the moment, so I'm not required to release my evidence."

"How can I defend myself if I don't know what you've got?"

"Relax, Jo," he said. "You're not being charged. It probably won't come to that, anyway. Just let us do our job and it'll all be over soon."

"This is a nightmare," she said. "What about my cattle?"

"The EPA and FDA investigators will be here later," Agent Harden said. "They'll be bringing a federal order impounding the cattle until we can be certain there is no contamination."

"And what do I do until all this is finished?"

"Just go on about your business," the agent said. "There's nothing else you can do."

But she couldn't even do that. With federal authorities tying up her business and camping on her doorstep, there was no aspect of her business that could possibly proceed normally. But instead of giving in to despair as many might have done, Jo got angry. There was no way these men were going to march into her life and force her to sit on the sidelines while they ordered her around. She wasn't the type to sit still for it and didn't intend to do so now.

She certainly wasn't the type to helplessly wait while the government built a charge of murder against her. Jo Tate wouldn't go down without a fight.

Chapter Eleven

Jo urged her horse into a gallop, letting the wind rushing over her face soothe away the heat of her anger as she put space between her and her ranch house. Only when she'd passed over the rise that took the ranch from sight did she allow the horse to slow to a trot and make its own way toward the stream that bisected her property. She didn't like being angry, but overworking her horse on a hot day was no way to overcome it.

There was no possible credible evidence that she had killed Norton Pettigrew, yet the authorities claimed to have some. That bothered her. It could only mean that someone was making an effort to cast the blame on her. This meant that she was the killer's intended second victim, and though her end may not be as permanent as the one Pettigrew had suffered, it was surely intended to be just as complete.

But who would be doing this to her? She was more than willing to believe that Zane had killed Pettigrew, but he wouldn't have been able to plant evidence against her. Not believable evidence, anyway. Unless he...no, she couldn't believe that Glen would go so far as to help frame her for the murder. Not even Glen was that low.

Was he? She couldn't be sure of anything now, not after Andrew had looked her in the eye and all but accused her of committing the crime.

Well, he hadn't actually accused her. She had to be fair to Andrew no matter how she felt. It was obvious that it hurt him to admit any suspicion at all, just as it was clearly obvious that he didn't believe the evidence that they did have.

Still, she had no idea what their evidence was.

Dan was flying north along the western edge of the slowly moving herd as she drew up on the cattle, the noise of his helicopter muffled and distant. From what she could see, he was doing an excellent job, eradicating all her previous fears about the effectiveness of aerial herding.

She watched him working the herd, and the rest of her anger was whisked away on the whirling blades of his chopper. She smiled, thinking of just how indispensable he was to her already. Even though it had only been a little over a week, she couldn't imagine life without the man.

With a man like Dan on her side, she couldn't imagine that anything would go wrong for long. Together, they would find the truth behind the murder and the chemical dumping. Together, they would overcome all obstacles.

Now they had only to overcome the obstacles to their love. Sitting astride the slowly trotting horse, Jo felt a need for him, a need greater than that which had propelled them toward her bedroom this morning. His nearness was a tantalizing reminder of how far away love seemed even when it was within reach. She wondered, with a wry smile, whether the FBI intended to lock her out of her bedroom as well as her office.

And that thought brought her mind back to the problems at hand. Someone was out to get her, and it was, therefore, no time to be dreaming of love. She couldn't imagine who might be doing this to her, or how any of it tied together with her neighbor's death or the deaths of the cattle, but she certainly wasn't going to wait idly while government investigators figured it out for her.

In fact, her present state of inactivity was beginning to grate on her. But she had a solution for that. She took the microphone of her portable radio in hand and keyed it on.

"Hello, flyboy," she said into the mike. "Jo here, over."

"Hi, boss. I'll set her down in a minute. Over and out."

Jo watched as the metal bird turned and swooped down toward the rise to the north of her. Moments later, it came to rest in the grass that flattened beneath its powerful breath, and Dan opened the canopy and stepped out.

"I'm not paying you to sit around," she said good-naturedly as she urged her horse toward him.

"I wasn't getting close enough contact up there," he explained as he reached up toward her. Then, with no more warning than his broadening smile, he grasped her hand and pulled her from her mount into his waiting arms.

His lips found hers, claiming them with an intensity that bespoke immense need and devotion. The pressure of those lips and the cradling arms around her brought the flame of her desire to a renewed heat that seared away all thought of work and worry. Nothing was impossible when she was in his arms, no task too arduous to complete.

Dan let her feet down to the ground, continuing to hold her body to his while maintaining the pressure of their bodies together. It was as though he was unwilling to part from her for even the moment needed to take a breath. When they did part, it was only for a moment and only as far as the few inches needed to look into each other's eyes.

But it was necessary for them to part, regretfully, if only to complete their work so that they could be together again. And Jo was the one who finally pushed away while every fiber of her being called out for her to stay in his arms.

"We can't carry on like this out in the open, Dan," she said. "The boys will see us."

"We've got a thousand head of cattle between us and them," he reminded her. "Miles and miles of cows and grass."

"And they've all got binoculars."

"Well, they can just mind their own business," he said, laughing. "Besides, they're bound to find out, anyway, aren't they? I don't know if I can go on hiding my affection for you. In fact, I feel like yelling about it from the nearest mountaintop."

"Oh, Dan, I feel the same way. I can't imagine not having you in my life—full-time."

Dan lowered his head, claiming her lips once more. This time their kiss was all the more sweet, after having declared their intentions to become a couple.

"Is this the whole reason you had to put down on the ground?" Jo asked him at last. "I'm not complaining, mind you, because I was thinking of doing just this. But I'm curious about your reasons."

"It was a strong motivation," Dan said, massaging the back of her hand with his thumb as he held it gently in his hand. "But it also occurred to me that our conversations aren't exactly private. The FBI has a whole bunch of scanners and such to listen in on our radio transmissions. I don't think we should be communicating in the clear while they're in the neighborhood."

"You're right," she admitted. "I hadn't thought of that, Dan. In fact, if they're listening, then it's also possible that whoever killed Pettigrew might be listening."

"So we'd better stick to cattle talk on the radio, boss," he said. "I wasn't sure what you wanted to tell me, but it seemed like a good idea to talk about it down here. You know, just in case it was something sensitive."

"It was. I was going to suggest that you take a spin over Pettigrew's main ranch and see what's going on over there. The FBI isn't even investigating that end of this thing. They're concentrating on me, instead. They claim to have some kind of evidence linking me to the murder."

"What? Has anyone told them that they're crazy?"

"I would imagine that countless people have told them that, but I have a feeling they're not listening."

"It figures. What did you want me to look for?"

"I don't know, but somebody should be keeping an eye on the Pettigrew ranch. Can you fly high enough so that no one notices you and you can still see details on the ground?"

"Sure, I've got good binoculars. But I don't have an autopilot on this thing," he said, indicating the waiting aircraft. "It's hard to fly and scout at the same time."

"It figures. Well, I suppose Dorothy will be all right down here for a few minutes. I'll go up with you."

"Dorothy?" Dan grinned, cocking his head quizzically.

"My horse," she explained, patting the patient animal's flank. "Dorothy Parker."

"Really?"

"Yes, is there something wrong with that?" Jo let the reins fall to the ground, which was just as good as tethering a trained horse.

"No, it's cool. I just never met a horse named Dorothy Parker before."

"I never met a Texan smart enough to fly a helicopter, either," she said, laughing. "Come on, let's go before I come to my senses. But I warn you," she said as they walked toward the craft, "you better keep this beast level or this budding relationship may be history."

AT THE HEIGHT they were flying, the Pettigrew ranch was nothing more than a collection of dark rectangles connected by brown lines in a sea of grass below them. Dan's binoculars, however, brought the scene close enough to make out people among the buildings below them. Jo watched intently as the crew went about their business much as her own crew was going about theirs.

"Nothing unusual," she said into the microphone of her headset. "Everything seems normal, and I don't see anything out of the ordinary at all."

"No big tanker trucks down there?" Dan asked as he held them hovering overhead. "What about outbuildings big enough to hold a truck?"

"Might hide one in the barn, of course, but I rather doubt it. They'd have to make room by taking something out. We'd see that."

"Do they have any other buildings? Maybe away from the main ranch?"

"A couple line shacks. Nothing big enough to hide a truck."

"Where are they? We should take a quick look while we're up here."

Dan followed her directions to the northwest, passing high over one of the small, one-room shacks the ranch maintained to store gear out on the range. The first one was vacant, showing no signs of habitation at all. The second, which was on much more remote territory, was not only occupied, but the very same tanker Dan had seen on the road the previous day was parked beside it.

"There we are," Jo exclaimed. "There's a tanker right there as plain as can be. Goodness, Daniel, that proves it."

"So let's call the cavalry," Dan suggested.

"I don't think that will work," she said thoughtfully. "This shack is just two miles off federal land. They could be off the ranch and headed away on the highway in a matter of minutes. It's at least an hour by car to this shack," she reminded him.

"It wouldn't do to blow the whistle only to come up empty," Dan agreed. "We've either got to catch them in the act or find a way to get the federal agents up here faster."

"It wouldn't be fast enough," she said. "Someone is getting into the truck now. Yes, they're moving it."

Jo watched as the truck pulled away from the shack and made its way east along one of the rutted paths through the grass. Following high overhead, they stuck with the moving vehicle for half an hour as it made its slow progress east toward her ranch. Finally, it reached the road it was on the other day, and there it met a battered pickup. The two vehicles proceeded north a short way and then off the road between the rise of two low hills. Then the driver of the truck got out and climbed into the pickup, which drove away to the south along the road.

"What are they doing?" Dan asked.

"They're leaving the truck there," she told him. "I wonder what...wait a minute, I bet I know what they're up to. They're only a mile off our land there. If the truck is found, we could easily be accused of driving it there."

"What if there are still chemicals in the truck?" Dan said. "They could put a stop to the whole thing if they can provide a source of the poison for those cattle. I think they're planning something."

"Right. I imagine they'll be out to retrieve that truck tonight, Dan. They'll have to dump the chemicals on my land near where we found the cattle if they want to make it stick. And they will have to do it real soon, too. The EPA and FDA people will be here tomorrow for sure."

"That's what they'll do then. And then it'll look like Pettigrew had gotten the goods on you, so you killed him to keep him quiet," Dan said.

"I will kill somebody if they pour their toxins onto my land," Jo said vehemently. "I'll shoot them dead."

"We should probably try to avoid that," Dan said wryly as he turned the helicopter toward Jo's waiting horse. Then he said forcefully, "Damn, I know what we should have done... Do you have a video camera?"

"Yes, why?"

"I should have thought of this before, Jo, but I can mount it beside the lights on the old gun rack outside the copter. We could have just swooped down on them when they were at the shack and gotten recorded evidence against them."

"I thought the weapons were taken off this thing," Jo said with trepidation.

"They are, but I've got the mechanism for turning them. There are floodlights on the gun swivels so that I can direct the beams wherever I want them."

"Okay, so we can still mount the camera on one of them and get footage tonight if they try anything."

"We sure can, boss. We'll have them all in jail by tomorrow afternoon if we're lucky."

"Damn lucky," she said. "You'd better put me down on the ground so that I can get Dorothy and then go find my video camera. You fly back to the ranch, and I'll meet you there."

"Okay." He brought the copter down about one hundred feet from where Dorothy Parker stood patiently nibbling grass near the western edge of the herd. "Maybe you should mention this to the feds," he said.

"No, I'm not ready to let them in on anything, Dan. And don't go up to the house," she warned him as she got out. "They've sealed off my office, and heaven knows what else they've taken command of around there. I'd rather not get any of those government types excited about us, or they might just go ahead and impound the copter before we get a chance to use it."

Jo watched him take off. He took a few passes at the herd to convince a few wandering cattle to return to the herd and then swung south and headed back to the ranch. Jo mounted her horse feeling more confident than she had half an hour earlier. If they were right about the dumpers' intentions, they should be able to spring a trap on them tonight.

The world around her seemed as vibrant and alive as ever as she rode back to the ranch. Nature seemed to be in command, the wind and water working to continue the miracle of life just as they always had. A week ago, she would never have thought of how close to the edge they really were. One evil man with nothing on his mind but an easy profit could easily poison the land so that it wasn't fit for use anymore. All it took was greed and a lack of conscience.

The thought angered her. She couldn't imagine anyone being like that. Even Norton Pettigrew had more sense, didn't he? Apparently not, for it was his greed that invited the men with their tanker of noxious chemicals up here to this pristine land. It was his shortsightedness that worked to poison the world that gave them life. And, ultimately, through some misstep, it was his own greed that led to his death. She supposed that in the end he'd gotten what was coming to him.

But now it was up to her and Dan to stop the cancerous flow of his greedy work. It wasn't just her own freedom and good name at stake; the sanctity of the land itself hung in the balance.

"The land is everything," her father had told her many times. "Without it we have nothing. If we don't take care of it, we're no better than ignorant apes who don't deserve the bounty we've taken from it."

She remembered his words now and vowed to hold them even more sacred in her heart. Nobody was going to get away with murdering the land. Nobody.

Miss TATE, we've come across something here."
Agent Harden stepped out of her office to confront her
as she was crossing from the front door toward the hall
to the bedroom. "Perhaps you'd like to explain it if you
can."

"What is it?" She was put on alert by the predatory
coldness of the man's icy eyes, and she followed him
warily to the office door. "Am I allowed in there?" she
asked him.

"Come in for a moment, if you would," he said.

Three men were seated at her father's large desk, one
working at her computer while the other two were busy
going through her papers. Agent Harden led her past
them, however, to one of the file cabinets against the
wall beneath several framed photographs of her parents working the ranch. A slip of notepaper lay alone on
top of the file cabinet, and it was toward this paper the
agent directed her attention.

"Have you seen this paper before?" he asked her seriously.

She reached to take it, but the agent motioned quickly
to stop her. "Don't touch the evidence," he said. "I
don't want you claiming that your fingerprints got on
today."

Jo moved up to the cabinet and read the wrinkled
sheet of paper with growing alarm.

*I'll meet you near the south road tonight. I'm sure
you don't want to have this talk where anyone can hear
us. Eleven o'clock.*

The note was written in longhand, and it was signed
by Norton Pettigrew.

"What's this about?" she asked.

"You've never seen this note before?"

"Of course not. Why would I be asking if I had?"

"It was on the floor between the cabinet and the trash can," Harden said. "It looks like you just missed throwing it away."

"Or someone wanted it to look that way," she countered.

"It's possible," he admitted. "But who would have had access to do that?"

"My intruder last night," she offered. "That might be why he was here."

"If there was an intruder."

"I've got witnesses," she insisted.

"All of them in your employ. That's not convincing. Can you think of anybody else who might have *planted* this note?"

"Nobody," she said. But then she paused, this morning's scene coming to mind. "Unless Deputy Sheriff Wright was in here this morning," she told him.

"You're saying that an officer of the law would try to frame you for Norton Pettigrew's murder."

"Yes, if you really want to define Glen Wright as an officer of the law, that's exactly what I'm saying. I didn't see him in here, personally. You would know better than I if he came in with your crew."

"That's quite an accusation, Miss Tate."

"Not if you knew Glen. Look, I'm not accusing him of anything at the moment. All I'm saying is that he's the only one I know of who might have had access to plant that note."

"What's his motive?"

"We have a long history of problems," she said, unwilling to go into such details of her personal life with the man. "For now, all I'm saying is that he might have done it, and that I wouldn't put it past him to have done it. And I sure as hell haven't seen that note before now."

"I'll check on the deputy," the agent said, allowing a small smile to slip onto his lips. "But until we prove otherwise, we'll have to go on the assumption that this note was written to you. We have to verify the handwriting, too."

"Well, it does like like his handwriting," she admitted. "There's no denying that."

"Okay," Harden said. "We're going to be very thorough on this matter. Nobody wants to railroad you, and I don't want you to think we're out to get you. We just have to be as complete as possible."

"I understand that, Agent Harden. But I haven't done anything wrong. Here you are going through my records when we all know damn well that nobody accepting payment for illegal dumping would put it on their ledger."

"Not the books you take to the accountant, no," he said. "But your home records are a different matter. You'd be surprised how many times suspects just couldn't resist tallying up illegal profits for their own records and just left it on their hard disk."

"So why aren't you checking into Norton Pettigrew's accounts? Why me?"

"As I told you earlier, his books are being checked by professional accountants right now. Furthermore, Miss Tate, the cattle were dead on your property. Norton Pettigrew was dead on your property. Now we find this note. We'd be fools if we didn't investigate you first."

"And you'll look like bigger fools if your investigating me turns out to be a wild-goose chase," she said hotly.

"Sure. And that's exactly why we're being so thorough. Now, if you'll step out of the office, we'll get on with our work."

Jo was, once again, ushered out of her own office and into the hall where the door was closed in her face. But this time she didn't need to feel impotent in the face of their official indifference. This time, she had an investigation of her own to carry out, and when it was finished, the agent would be singing an entirely different tune.

Chapter Twelve

Hank Driscoll and the other hands of the Bar T Ranch listened intently as Dan outlined the plan. The pilot had flown directly out to where the wranglers were finishing up their work on the fence line after he and Jo had secured the video camera on the swivel mount beside the right floodlight.

"No more radio transmission," he told the men gathered around his helicopter. "We don't know who's listening, so there's no sense in taking chances."

"Nobody is listening," Hank proclaimed sourly. "And Andrew isn't going to arrest Jo because of some fabricated evidence the FBI came up with. The two of you are getting all paranoid here, is all."

"Well, somebody planted that note in Jo's office," Dan countered. "I think a bit of paranoia is pretty well advised in this case, Hank."

"Hell, it was Glen that put the note there," David said adamantly. "We all know that. He just doesn't want Jo to have anything good without him, so he's making life rough on her. He's been making all our lives miserable since she turned him down two years back."

"Prove it," Dan said. "That's not so easy. I'm sure they'll give Jo a break if they can, but they've got procedure to stick to and they sure aren't going to deviate from that on the word of their prime suspect. It's up to us to prove this thing. And even if we tell the authorities, the odds are that they won't do anything soon enough to do us any good. They'll have to dump that stuff tonight so it has some time to soak in before the EPA finds it."

"I don't like the idea of riding the horses out there at night," Hank said. "Endangering the horses over some fool idea that probably won't pan out is stupid."

"You just want to go to town and moon after Mary Montgomery," Bill ribbed him. "You're afraid Zane will cart her off somewhere when you aren't looking."

"No, I'm afraid that if I don't break your nose for you, somebody else will beat me to the punch," the foreman replied. "I just don't like this little plan of yours, flyboy. Hell, you may be right for all I know, but I just don't like it."

"I think Zane will be here with the truck anyway," Dan mentioned. "It would probably take at least two of them. You would have noticed if they had too many people up here. The town's just not that big."

"That's as may be," Hank said, "but it's still a stupid plan to drag horses out on the prairie in the dead of night."

The foreman regarded Dan with open suspicion then, and Dan was suddenly aware of how he had bypassed Hank in this matter. Of course the man didn't like the plan—he hadn't been consulted. Dan knew now it was a mistake to have come out to the range without Jo. The men would do anything for her, but Dan was still just another hired hand to them.

None of that could be helped now. Jo hadn't wanted it to look suspicious to the federal agents, because if they were forced to divulge the plan to the agents, it wouldn't be long before the deputy was informed, too. If Glen was in on the crime, he would surely alert the polluters. So Jo had decided against coming with him for fear that her voluntary flight in the helicopter would look suspicious to Andrew.

"It's not my plan, really," Dan said, backtracking. "Besides, there should be enough moonlight for your horses to find their footing. We just want you boys to stick close to where you found the dead cattle so you can be ready to rush the dumpers."

"Which place?" Jay asked. "Pettigrew's cattle were about twenty miles south of where we found our dead cows."

"They left the truck well north of here," Dan said. "I'm betting they'll dump between the two sites. Probably in a gully that won't look too conspicuous but won't be hard to find, either. Do you guys know of a likely spot for them to do it? I have no idea."

"There's a small creek up there," Bill offered. "It's dry now, but it runs pretty full in the spring. There's always good grass along the banks."

"Okay, so I think we can safely assume that's where they'll head."

"It would make a good spot," Hank said, bowing to the argument behind their plan for the night. "That creek runs into Pettigrew property. That would have given Norton a good reason to be mad at Jo. If threats were made and all, I can see where some fool law officer might think she got mad and killed him."

"A perfect reason," Dan agreed. "We just have to be ready for them."

"Well, if they're going to back some big old truck in there, they're going to want moonlight," Hank mused out loud. "The moon won't be up till after midnight. I'd guess about one or one-thirty for their move."

"So maybe we ought to get some rest now," Bill said. "This could take all night."

"Good idea," Hank said. "Except that, of course, we'll have to go into town tonight, anyway."

"Why?" Dan asked. "We've got more important things to do."

"Sure, but we can't change our habits, can we? It might tip them off."

"You boys don't go into the bar every night, do you?"

"No," Hank said. "Except that David got himself arrested by Glen Wright last night. Anybody who knows us will expect the bunch of us to be in town tonight just to rub Glen's nose in the fact that David isn't sitting in jail. You tell Jo we're going to go to town for supper tonight. She'll understand."

"You could avoid that macho crap just once, couldn't you?" Dan saw nothing but trouble in that plan. They needed a full crew on the range to catch the dumpers, and all he saw ahead of them in town was a fight.

"Nobody trumps up charges against one of the Bar T crew and gets away with it," Bill said. "Hank's right. Most everybody in town will be waiting for us to crack Glen a good one. Or," he added, smiling, "at least come to town and act like stupid cowboys for a couple hours."

"Well, then get some rest before you go in," Dan said reluctantly. "And don't you boys do any drinking. This is important."

"Yes, Mommy," David said, laughing.

"I know what's important," Hank said firmly. "We're the ones who will be on the ground in range of any weapons they might have along while you're up out of the fray. None of us is going to put our safety in jeopardy."

"I'll have to be a little closer than that if I want to get pictures," Dan said. "If past experience is any indication, I suspect I'll be the one drawing fire."

"Well, in that case," Hank said, "maybe I do like your plan, after all."

DAN WAS ALONE in the bunkhouse. Shirtless in a pair of running shorts, he was carefully going through the practice movements of tae kwan do, executing a series of kicks and punches as a fine sheen of sweat grew on his torso. The exercise, involving several ritual balanced poses between flurries of blinding kicks, always served to calm his spirit as well as train his body. He found a focus in the regimen, a concentration of mind and body afforded him by no other activity, and he turned to the exertion and routine of his training exercises whenever he needed to prepare himself for demanding activity.

He'd started in martial arts when he was a teenager while still recovering from the fall that had left his body so badly scarred. The discipline had toned his body and given him his confidence back after a long convalescence. Now, holding third-degree black belts in both tae kwan do and karate, he credited most of his success to the inner strength he'd gained through the training. He had found that the best way to avoid a fight was to be confident enough to back away from it.

Of course, once struck, all his training told him to make certain that he wasn't struck again. That was what had happened in town the other night. He would have preferred not to have put on such a display in public, because people often get the wrong impression from such things. But when Zane struck him, Dan's training took over until the man was down, the danger passed. Fortunately, this was a western town. A person's ability to defend himself was still valued here, and so the brief fight was allowed to pass without undue notice. It probably helped, too, that Ken Zane already had a reputation as a scuffler and that nobody was particularly sympathetic toward him.

A board creaked behind him, and Dan spun swiftly, landing profile to the door with his hands up and ready. Jo smiled from the doorway, nodding as she entered the spare and tidy room.

"Don't mind me," she said, taking a seat in the chair just inside the door. "I'll just sit here a while and relax while I enjoy the view."

"I'm about done," he told her as he pushed a tendril of sweat-dampened hair back from his forehead. "I haven't practiced the past couple days."

"What is that? Karate?" The play of the taut muscles in the man's upper body mesmerized her, each one lean yet clearly defined beneath his glistening skin. She was struck by the urge to run her hand over the washboard expanse of his muscled stomach.

"Tae kwan do," he said. He executed a series of punches against an imaginary opponent, then spun and kicked.

"That's a kind of karate, right? You didn't go into too much detail before."

"It's Korean," he explained as he continued the exercises. "Karate is Japanese."

"Is there a difference?"

"To the Koreans there is." Dan laughed, stopping to take a towel and wipe his face. "Tae kwan do is mostly kicking. Very stylized. Karate uses the hands more. You know, breaking boards and that stuff."

"But you were punching, too," she said.

"Yeah, well I mix styles. Actually, I've trained in both forms with some kempo and kick boxing thrown in. Like I said, it's American karate. A lot of tae kwan do practitioners are useless with their hands. Once you get close enough, you've got them. Kick boxing teaches you to keep your guard up," he said. "Would you like to learn?"

"It looks like too much work."

"It is, I suppose." Dan walked to her and touched the side of her face, unable to avoid making contact. "But you learn to focus your energies. And you can avoid a lot of fights by knowing how to fight."

"I don't expect to get into many fights," she said. "Nothing I'd have to punch my way out of, anyway."

"A woman should know how to defend herself. And, if you're going to defend yourself, you have to be able to do it automatically. If you take time to think, it'll be too late."

"Like the other night in the bar?"

"I was a bit slow on the rebound," Dan said, "but, yes, just like that." Dan walked over and sat on the couch, watching the woman across the room with adoring eyes. "Martial arts is a philosophy as much as anything else. You never strike the first blow, and you always avoid any fight if you can. But, if attacked, you stop the attack however you have to."

"That sounds rather final," Jo said. "What do you mean, however you have to?" She walked over and sat beside him on the couch.

"Well, to put it bluntly, the best way to keep some one from continuing an attack is to break their bones." Dan laughed. "You know, in the movies you see tough guys punching each other in the face like fools until someone falls down. In real life, you'd break your knuckles a lot sooner than you'd knock the other guy down. Ribs are better targets, and elbows or feet are better weapons."

"Especially if you happen to be wearing a pair of cowboy boots," Jo said as she leaned on his shoulder and reached up to trace her finger down the side of his cheek.

"It would help," he said, staring down at his own bare feet. "I'm afraid I've got myself all lathered up here," he said. "I should go take a shower so I don' smell like a horse."

"You don't," she assured him. "But then, maybe you need someone to scrub your back."

"Well, maybe I do." He kissed her lightly. "And we could take a little nap before our big night."

"We could try," she said, tipping her head to kiss his throat. "Though I doubt we'll do much sleeping."

"So do I." This was too much, and Dan couldn't stand another minute of it, so he pushed her gently away. "I hope we can use your shower," he said. "The boys will be in soon to get prettied up before they go to town."

"They're going in tonight?" She sat back then, allowing the change of topic to cool some of her ardor.

"Yes, Hank said to tell you they'd be taking supper in town. It's something about the honor of the ranch after last night's run-in with Glen."

"Well, I suppose it would look odd if they didn't show up to act like big children after that," she allowed. "Just as long as they don't get themselves arrested, I don't suppose it can hurt anything."

"So far as I know, that's not on their agenda."

"Of course, that does mean that they won't be hanging around the ranch tonight, doesn't it?"

"Now that the feds are gone for the night, we'll have the place to ourselves," he said.

"So why are we sitting here?" Jo bounded up from the couch. "The last one to the house has to cook supper."

She ran from the bunkhouse while Dan paused briefly to grab the clothing he had laid out earlier to change into after his workout. By the time he left his quarters, she was already in the living room pulling off her boots.

They hurried through to the master bathroom, passing the yellow police tape secured across the office door without a second thought to the problems that ribbon of plastic represented. Their thoughts were consumed by each other, thoughts completely controlled by the passion that brought them into each other's arms while the running water began to steam up the room around them.

Jo was as good as her word, scrubbing his back with tender care and sealing her work with kisses across his strong shoulders. The sparkling flow of hot water further heightened their passion as they held each other beneath the spray and let their hands tease and explore while lips and tongues moved to savor everything about their bodies. His delicate touches brought her to the quivering edge, blowing her thoughts away to a land of sparkling sensations as she arched back to kiss him, hold him and return the gift of his love.

It was a delicious experience to be together like this, sharing everything as they neared the consummation that was only a touch, a movement away. But that consummation wasn't to take place in a shower, no matter how large and luxurious it might be. No, their love wanted space and time to achieve the physical communion they so ardently desired. Jo turned off the hot water, and they began to towel each other off, only to give up the effort and fall into each other's arms once more.

Dan carried her into the bedroom, his muscles taut against her bare skin as their lips remained joined, refusing to give up the contact until they could at last collapse onto the bed and wrap themselves around each other. She grasped and pulled him to her with eager hands, engulfing and surrounding him as her body accepted his body and they became one moving sensation.

This, yes, this was it. The heat of the day was banished, and the sun itself seemed to have disappeared from the sky as Jo gave her body over to the explosion of fulfillment that burst within her. It seemed to take only seconds for them both to reach the pinnacle of feeling that they had been denied too many times before. That fulfillment, that sated desire, built into another, greater desire, and Jo rolled to rise up and take his body as she had allowed herself to be taken, both of them rushing to yet another crescendo of love.

At last they lay together, nestled in bed like two pieces of a jigsaw puzzle. And they knew the realization of their love just as they knew that it was theirs forever.

Jo EMERGED from their second bath—a luxurious, playful soaking rather than the impetuous rush of their earlier shower. She walked through the bedroom wrapped in one of her large towels and toweling her hair dry with another, looking for the man who had emerged before her.

"There you are," she said, finding him in the den standing beside the gun case and looking up at the trophy wall.

He looked so perfectly at home standing there with the towel wrapped around his waist, his torso naked and still slightly damp from the tub. He looked so right standing there, she felt as though he'd been a part of her life forever.

"You have quite a collection here," he commented.

Dan nodded toward the many ribbons and trophies that filled the wall and the top of the bookcase. It had been her father's favorite place, the one location he was certain to take any new visitor to look at his little girl's accomplishments.

"I guess I did all right," Jo said modestly as she slipped up beside him and put her arm around his waist. "My father was always embarrassing me by taking people in here and showing them the trophies. It didn't matter who they were. Feed salesmen, cattle buyers, it didn't matter. The first order of business was to show them the wall."

"That didn't really embarrass you, though, did it?"

"No, I guess not."

"He had a lot to be proud of," Dan said. "And I don't mean just riding." He kissed her, leaning his head down to share the sweet pressure of her lips for a moment.

"It feels real good to make your father proud," she said. "Doesn't it?"

"Oh, yes." Dan looked back at the wall, holding her shoulder gently against his side. "My father is a stickler for accuracy in his work. Every T is crossed, every I dotted properly. But he has one hell of a sense of humor. My flying was always a miracle of sorts to him. I remember one time, we had some kind of political barbecue at my uncle's ranch. I was flying out there from college, and I got there during the middle of the thing. Well, I took the fool notion that it might be fun to see how low I could come in over those people lined up at the tables with their plates in hand."

"You didn't!" Jo said.

"Oh, yes, I sure did," Dan replied. He laughed recalling the moment. "I couldn't have been more than ten feet off the ground when I crossed the grills. And I managed to just nudge the top of the big canopy they had in the yard for shade. It was a wonderful feat of sheer piloting stupidity. And all those people in their sport coats and spring dresses hitting the dirt."

"What happened? Your father couldn't have reacted well to that."

"He dressed me down when I landed, that's for sure," Dan admitted. "But I'd been reprimanded a time or two in my life, Jo, and I could tell it was just for show. There was a twinkle in his eyes, you see, like he was laughing inside. He was proud of the way I could handle the plane, and the nerve I showed for pulling such a stunt at all. A couple years later, he admitted that all those people diving for cover was the funniest thing he'd ever seen in his life."

"That is an odd sense of humor," Jo agreed.

"It's not a real good example, I suppose, but I know what you mean about making your father proud. He was there for every tae kwan do or karate competition

I ever entered. I remember him sitting in the audience, grinning and shouting, and twisting his program up in a tight knot the whole time. He never pushed me, though. Not even back when I was still—"

Dan's story broke off abruptly, dissolving into a pensive expression knitting his eyebrows.

"When you were what?" Jo coaxed.

"When I was still riding," he said. "I used to be on horseback quite a bit. Nothing like you, Jo, no first-place trophies. I did get second place at the county fair once, but my brother was the trophy winner in the family."

"What happened? Why don't you ride now?"

"I told you I fell through a window," he said. "We were interrupted before I had a chance to explain that to you."

Dan cleared his throat, pausing to find the memory and the words to explain it.

"We were at the ranch getting ready to ride into town for the Fourth of July parade. I was fourteen years old. I was in the saddle waiting for my brother to get done talking to the girls and ride in with me. My younger cousins were out throwing firecrackers around—at one another mostly—and one of them tossed a lit package of black cats in the yard. It kind of skipped under my horse and started exploding."

Jo held him tighter, nestling her head against his chest and knowing what happened now. She could already imagine the horror of the event.

"I wasn't ready, you see," Dan went on. "The reins flew out of my hand and the horse leaped over the picket fence toward the house, trying to get away from the explosions. We went through the picture window before I even knew what happened. When I woke up, I was in a hospital and it was nearly a week later.''

"Oh, God, Dan, that's terrible," Jo whispered.

"They had to shoot the horse right there in the front room to stop him from kicking me while he died. I was torn open, and my mother damn near died seeing me like that, but they got me into town in time to keep me going.

"I remember my parents sitting beside the bed, my father especially, just sitting there watching me. He didn't read or do any work but just sat there for hours, watching and putting on a smile whenever I opened my eyes. I was in the hospital for three months and he was always there whenever I woke up.

"I think he enjoyed my little aerial stunt, because flying was as close as I ever got to getting back on the horse after falling off. It proved that I hadn't lost my nerve. I just didn't want to ride anymore.''

"You never rode again?"

"No, not until last night." Dan shrugged. "I don't really know why not, either. I was three months in the hospital and missed most of the next year of school. When I did go back, my muscles were still atrophied, and I was underweight. I wasn't really strong enough to ride. Martial arts were therapy to get me back in shape. Tae kwan do was my horse.''

"Well, that was some pretty fine riding last night," she said. "Maybe we'll get you up on one again."

"It is hard to work a ranch without riding some-time," he admitted. "But I keep thinking of that poor horse. It's really silly to be worried about riding now."

"Oh, I love you," Jo said, encircling him with her arms.

"And I love you." He kissed her, holding her tightly to him. "I think we have a few minutes, too," he said. "I have a powerful hankering for your lovely young body, Ms. Tate."

"Oh, Mr. Fitzpatrick," Jo said, giggling. "Right here in Daddy's den? Why, he's liable to shoot you if he—"

Jo cut herself off, looking over Dan's shoulder as he pulled her towel down, caressing her shoulders. She was frozen, staring past him at the tall cabinet in the corner and the shiny barrel of a rifle visible through the glass doors.

"My, God," she whispered. "I know what their evidence against me is! The gun! My father's shotgun is missing!"

Chapter Thirteen

"My father had two rifles and a shotgun," Jo insisted as she gathered her towel around her and strode over to the gun cabinet. "The shotgun is gone now. See, you can see an outline in the dust from where the stock rested on the bottom of the cabinet."

She took a key from atop the cabinet and unlocked the door to point at the oval of clear wood exposed in the fine layer of dust coating the interior of the cabinet.

"I haven't had this case open in years," she told him. "Not even my father used the guns much, and they are the only ones we own."

"I'll bet that's what your intruder was up to," Dan said. "He was trying to put the shotgun back."

"Right," Jo answered ruefully. "I leave the house open most of the time. He could have stolen it anytime he wanted to, but he had trouble getting in to replace it. That's what he was carrying, probably wrapped in a gun bag."

"Well then, we know what they have on you, and we know that it isn't much. I don't think they'll ever find a jury around here that would be willing to convict you on this evidence."

"But it's keeping them off the right track, isn't it? Goodness, Dan, it could have been anyone who came in here and took the gun. I don't remember the last time I even looked at this case. They could have done it at any time."

"You should call the sheriff and tell him," Dan said.

"But he already knows about the gun," Jo countered. "Why bother calling."

"Just to be able to put a time on your discovery that the gun was missing," he said. "If this goes to court, the police will have a record of your call to report the theft."

"Just to be certain that we've crossed all the T's and dotted all the I's?"

"It couldn't hurt."

They left the den, returning to the bedroom once more. But, before Jo could pick up the phone, the doorbell rang.

"Oh, no," Jo said. She threw off her towel and slipped into her bathrobe, checking her hair quickly in the mirror. "I'll get rid of whoever it is," she promised.

"I'll be waiting."

But when Jo looked through the front window, she realized that it would probably be more than a minute. Andrew Hollander stood outside in his uniform looking grim.

Jo took a moment to cinch the belt on her white, terry-cloth robe tighter. Then she took a deep breath and opened the door.

"Hello, Andrew," she said calmly. "I was just about to call you, and I think you know why already."

"No, why was that?"

"My father's shotgun is missing. That's your evidence, isn't it?"

"Yeah," the lawman drawled, pushing his hat back on his head. "We found it up the draw from the body."

"That was awfully sloppy of me to leave it so close to where I killed Pettigrew, wasn't it?" she asked somberly. "I must be awfully stupid."

"Ah, Jo, you know I don't think you did it."

"You just figured it was smart to leave me hanging in the breeze, right?"

"No, I figured it wasn't good to look like a hick lawman in front of the FBI fellas. The law can't play favorites, Jo, and you know that."

"No, I suppose not," she admitted. "Well, I'm reporting the gun missing, Andrew. I just noticed it a moment ago. I figure the intruder was trying to put it back last night when I interrupted him. But, what brings you out here?"

"I'm looking for Dan Fitzpatrick, actually. Do you know where he is?"

"Why do you want him?" she asked quickly, her heart suddenly sinking. "He couldn't possibly have done anything wrong."

"I can't really say, Jo," the officer said, clearly uncomfortable. "It's official business, and I just can't tell you."

"Here we go again. You people are pretty good at keeping folks from answering to the charges against them, aren't you?" Jo said hotly. "This secrecy is stupid."

"Give me a break, Jo, I've got federal agents all over the place. If I had cut you some slack, it would have been me riding the barbed wire for it. Dan will have a chance to answer to the charges, if there are any. I just want to know where he is."

"I'm his employer, Andrew. Maybe I don't want to tell you where he is."

"Then I'll have to haul you in for obstructing justice, Jo. You don't want that, do you?"

"I want to know why you're after Dan. That's what I want to know."

"And I'm not going to tell you," the sheriff replied.

"Then tell me and get it over with," Dan said solidly as he walked into the living room.

He had dried himself and dressed quickly, doing his best to make his wet hair look as though he was wearing hair oil. But a drip of water that ran down in front of his right ear gave him away, and the sheriff looked from one to the other with dawning comprehension.

"So, that's how it is," he said. It seemed at that moment that a bit of the life left his eyes, as though the glimmer of hope he'd had for winning Jo Tate's affections had finally been extinguished.

"Yes," Dan said, "that's how it is." He slipped his arm around Jo's shoulders protectively.

Jo saw the change in Andrew's eyes and felt a twinge of guilt for it.

"You've only known each other a little over a week." Andrew cleared his throat, shifting from one foot to the other. "I hope you're not rushing into anything, Jo."

"I know what I want, Andrew. I've had plenty of time to figure it out."

The young sheriff pursed his lips and looked at them for a moment. He seemed to be considering his options. After a few more tense moments, he announced his decision by smiling tightly and holding his hand out to Dan. "You're one hell of a lucky cowboy," he said at last.

"That I am," Dan agreed. "Thank you."

"So, what in hell were you doing going through Norton Pettigrew's wallet?" Andrew asked sternly, getting back to the matter at hand. "Your fingerprints are all over it."

"Oh, that," Dan said, grimacing. "Well, I guess I got bored waiting."

"Waiting." Andrew spoke slowly, his eyes narrowed in thought. "So that means you went looking through the wallet while Hank was fetching me."

"Yes, that's correct," he admitted.

"So you were in on it too, Jo?"

"You've got me there, Andrew," she said.

"What on God's green earth is wrong with you people?" he expounded, his eyes darting between them. "Just because this is your land doesn't mean you can just go ahead and fiddle with anything you find lying around on it. This is murder! Don't you understand that?"

"Sure, I—" Dan began.

"What you understand doesn't really matter," Andrew interrupted. "It's Jo I'm worried about. What did you gain by going through the contents of Pettigrew's wallet?"

"Just some phone numbers, Andrew. That's all," Jo said. "But it does tie everything together somewhat. Or haven't you gotten around to calling the numbers yet?"

"Me? I haven't called anybody," the officer said. "And now that I've got EPA investigators in town, I can barely get into my office anymore. If the two of you had given some thought to the dead cattle when you found Norton's body, you might have realized that it would become a federal case. You're an army boy, too," he said to Dan. "You should have known the feds would have your prints in no time."

"I was rather hoping they'd overlook the wallet," he said.

"I sure would have," Andrew said. "It costs money to check prints, and Pettigrew wasn't robbed. But the FBI doesn't count pennies for fingerprints. They ran every flat surface for prints and a few of the rocks, as well. Now you're in a heap of trouble and Jo looks more guilty than ever."

"Okay, we're sorry," Jo said. "Look, I'll get dressed and then we can sit down and discuss this over a cup of coffee. Does that sound all right, or do you have to haul us in?"

"They've left it up to my discretion," he said. "And I think that a cup of coffee sounds damn good about now."

"Okay. Dan, you go brew a pot," she said. "I won't be a minute."

The two men walked to the kitchen where Andrew took a chair and sat straddling the back of it, his gun bobbing conspicuously in its holster at his side. He watched Dan fill the coffeemaker with water and measure out four heaping scoops of coffee to brew. Only when Dan had finished did the officer speak his mind.

"So it's you and Jo, huh?" he said. He took a long, slow breath, as though he was fighting to control his emotions. "I guess I can live with that. But I'll tell you one thing. If you cause her any grief, I'll kill you."

"You're the second man here who's given me that warning," Dan said lightly.

"Maybe, but I'm very serious. I've known her since grade school, and loved her at least that long, and I'm not going to see her hurt."

"I won't hurt her, Hollander. But you could help her out a lot yourself, you know. Point the feds in the right direction on this thing before all their evidence goes south on them. Pettigrew was the one doing the dumping."

"There is no evidence against him, Dan," the sheriff said. The tone of his voice displayed a clear desire to find such evidence, and dismay at his failure to do so. "Hell, I'd make it up if I could."

"I believe you, Sheriff." Dan stood up and got three cups from the cupboard, removing the carafe to hold one beneath the coffee running out through the filter. "But if you follow through on those phone numbers in Pettigrew's wallet, you'd probably find plenty of evidence. Hell, we've been able to draw some pretty good conclusions from them ourselves."

"I don't have any phone numbers," Andrew said.

"You must. There was a card for a New Jersey chemical hauler and a separate slip of paper that had the owner's private line listed. Both New Jersey numbers."

"There was nothing in his wallet but money and credit cards. No phone numbers."

"None at all?" Jo exclaimed from the kitchen door.

"Damn!" Dan cried out as coffee brimmed over the forgotten cup and onto his fingers. He replaced the carafe quickly and ran cold water over his thumb. "Maybe it's lucky you found my fingerprints, after all, Sheriff, or you might never have followed this thing up."

"You're sure about this?" Andrew asked.

"We both saw them," Jo said as she walked over to the sink to look at Dan's hand. "You'll live," she said to him, kissing his reddened thumb. "They were in the wallet."

The sheriff paused, thinking. "Then this investigation was hamstrung from the start, wasn't it?" he said quietly.

"Glen Wright," Dan said definitely.

"Maybe. You two had better fill me in on everything," he said. "And don't leave anything out."

Jo and Dan began at the point where they came upon Hank waiting by Norton Pettigrew's body and continued through their search and subsequent findings. The sheriff listened attentively, copying down the telephone number of the chemical disposal company and asking several questions along the way. He didn't stop their narrative, however, even when it was apparent that the law officer in him objected to their circumvention of the law.

"That's all of it?" Andrew asked when they'd finished. "He had the number of a chemical disposal firm in New Jersey, but they don't work in Montana?"

"Right, but they referred us to Great Sky Hauling," Jo insisted. "And Ken Zane handles Great Sky as one of his accounts."

"You're sure?"

"Yes, Hank remembered that. When he first came to the area, Zane visited every ranch to introduce his full line. He sells for several companies."

"And here I hadn't thought he sold much of anything," Andrew commented. "All he's done that I could see was drink beer and pick fights."

"So, if he isn't working at sales, maybe he's got a more profitable line," Dan said. "He'll stay until they're done dumping here and then move on to new territory."

"And he's become an awfully good friend of Glen's," Andrew mentioned, stroking his knuckle against his chin. "God, I hate to see Glen mixed up in this."

"It couldn't be anyone else," Jo said. "I hate to see it, too, but then he's always preferred the easy road to any other."

"Yes, and he's come close to losing his job a time or two," Andrew admitted. "Well, if this plays out as you expect it to, this'll be his last day on the county payroll, that's for sure."

"What do you think, Sheriff," Dan asked. "Will they be dumping tonight?"

"If they want the EPA investigators to find anything, they'll have to. Investigators will be all over your place tomorrow, so it'll be too late after that."

"And it will have to be dumped close to where both sets of cattle were found," Jo said.

"According to what Uncle Evan told me, the cows couldn't have gone far after they ate this stuff. It probably took half an hour to kill them. No more."

"Will you join our hunting party, then?" Jo asked.

"You'd better have someone with common sense along with you, that's for certain," Andrew said, laughing. "We'd better meet about midnight so we can be in place by moonrise."

"Right." Jo stood, putting her cup aside in the sink. "Meanwhile, my crew is in town putting on a macho show for your deputy's benefit."

"That's about their speed." Andrew took his hat from the table, standing. "I'll send them on home," he said, then paused before adding, "I'm not going to tell Agent Harden about this for now. He can make a fuss if he wants to, I suppose, but this is my jurisdiction, after all. It'll just be me, 'cause I don't want my other deputies to act any differently and tip Glen off.''

"Good. We'll be here at midnight," Jo said, glancing up at the clock above the sink. "And that's already less than two hours from now. We've been talking quite a while."

"Time flies when you're having fun," Dan commented.

"Okay, I'll head into town and send your crew out. I'll be back by midnight."

When he left them alone at last, the passion that had driven them earlier had dissipated, turned into nervous tension over the coming night's events. There was too much to be done to allow for love. But they would labor in the knowledge that everything they did would be to ensure their freedom, to share their love forevermore.

They had only to survive the coming night.

Chapter Fourteen

As Sheriff Hollander was starting on his journey back into town, Hank Driscoll was accepting a glass of rye whiskey from the bartender. He had mediated a tense situation between David and Glen at the diner earlier and had kept things in line up until the moment Mary Montgomery walked into the bar on Ken Zane's arm. The big guy dropped a possessive smile across his face as he passed Hank, winking at him as though they had something in common. Then he had taken Mary to a table in the center of the room, where he proceeded to ignore her for the evening.

Hank watched impotently. He knew full well he couldn't take the man in a fair fight, just as he knew that he couldn't afford to get busted up. Jo was counting on him tonight.

But he couldn't stand watching them together. That big bully with his smug look and pocketful of cash was treating Mary like garbage. Even from across the room he could see the hurt growing on her face with each of the little insults that Ken loved to throw her way in public.

Well, he told himself, *she made her bed and now she's got to lie in it.* But he turned toward the bar and ordered a drink, nonetheless, just to dull the pain of the sight. Hank Driscoll knew all about love, and as far as he could see, love was a botched job from the get-go.

Three glasses of rye and a beer later, Hank turned to watch them again. The whiskey had made him angry. If Jo and that pilot could be happy together, why couldn't he and Mary be happy? Didn't they deserve it as much as Jo? And, even if it wasn't to be him, didn't Mary deserve better than Ken Zane?

Hank wasn't thinking that if all went well later, Ken would be in jail by this time tomorrow night. No, that fact didn't occur to him at all when he pushed himself away from the bar and walked toward the table with his fists clenched.

"Zane," he growled. "I think maybe it's time I knocked you down a peg."

Ken laughed, his even, white teeth flashing in the low lights of the bar. They looked like such a good target that Hank struck them without waiting for the man to stand, smashing his fist into Ken's mouth with all his weight behind it and knocking the man over onto the floor.

Then pain shot through Hank's arm as his nerves alerted him to the fact that he'd cut his fingers on Zane's teeth and broken the knuckle of his little finger on the man's jaw. He grasped his hand in the other, wincing, as Ken stood, apparently, none the worse for wear.

"Okay, cowboy, knock me down," Ken taunted.

"No, Hank," Mary exclaimed, standing. "Get out of here."

"Shut up!" Ken pushed her back, knocking her over her chair to the floor.

Hank charged him blindly then, barreling headfirst into him with both arms swinging only to meet Zane's ready fists and ascending knee. He fought valiantly but was overpowered and only saved from a severe beating by the arrival of the rest of the Bar T crew from various other parts of the large bar.

They pulled him away, but the damage was done by then, and Hank was nauseated from the cumulative effects of the liquor he'd drunk, the broken finger and a swelling cut above his right eye.

Ken laughed, watching the three wranglers sit Hank down on a chair to minister to his wounds. "Come on, Mary," he said. "Let's get out of here."

"No." Mary Montgomery backed away from Zane, a look of fear and loathing in her eyes. "You leave me alone."

"I said, come on, woman." He made a move to get her, but this time he was stopped by the Bar T crew, who had resolved, to a man, to finish what their foreman had begun.

They charged him as a group, knocking him to the ground where Jay and Bill pinned him down while David began pummeling his stomach with his eager fists.

"Hey! Enough!" An authoritative voice cut through the excited noise of the gathering crowd, and Glen Wright stepped through in uniform with his gun drawn. "I'm going to haul the bunch of you in," he shouted. "Now get off that man."

"We were just helping him up," Bill said to the deputy.

"Yeah," said David, "he fell down."

"Like hell," Glen said, smiling. "Come on down to the office with me and we'll sort this all out. You boys have caused too much trouble around here for one night. I'll just let you spend the night on ice to cool off."

"Oh, shut up, Glen." Hank grabbed a beer bottle from the table beside him and clubbed the deputy over the back of the head with it. "Okay, boys," he said when the man fell senseless to the ground, "let's go home."

"Why don't you people stop them?" Ken was rising painfully, holding his stomach as he pulled himself to his feet. "They attacked me. They just knocked out an officer of the law!" he shouted to the onlookers. "Aren't you going to stop them?"

One by one, the other men and women in the bar returned to their own conversations and ignored his pleas as the Bar T crew walked out the door.

"That felt good," David said as they walked toward Hank's car. "Real good."

"Andrew will string us up tomorrow," Bill commented. "But I guess it did feel kind of good tonight."

"Was that some kind of new dance you boys were practicing in there?"

The four men turned quickly, facing the sheriff who had been seated patiently on the sill of the front window of the bar. He was frowning, shaking his head.

"How's that, Sheriff?" Hank asked.

"I don't know." Andrew pushed off the sill and walked to them. "It looked like you were dancing with Glen or something. Hope it doesn't catch on. It looked tiring."

"Yeah," David said, laughing. "Glen is still tuckered out."

"Like I said," Andrew warned levelly, moving to stand just inches in front of the grinning young wrangler, "I hope you don't plan to do much more of that kind of dancing around here. Now get out of here before someone forces me to do something about it."

The sheriff turned and walked into the bar withou
another word.

"I'D SWEAR they had it planned," David was saying a
they got out of the car before the bunkhouse. "Ken get
into a fight, and Glen is right there to arrest us."

"Of course they planned it, you darn fool," Hank
replied. "And we walked into it like children."

"Walked into what?" Jo emerged from the bunk
house, where she and Dan had been waiting for the mer
to return. It was just before midnight, and they were
becoming anxious about any delays.

"A little ruckus," Hank said quickly. "Nothing
much."

"Nothing much? You should've seen it, Jo. Hank
laid old Glen out with a bottle. Knocked him out cold."

"Are you boys drunk?" Jo demanded. She stalked
down from the porch of the bunkhouse toward the men
by the car. "Or are you just crazy?"

"We're not drunk," Bill said. "Probably crazy."

"Well, I guess you must be if you were fighting with
a deputy sheriff on a night when we've got important
things to do. I swear, sometimes I think you don't have
a brain among the bunch of you. And you, Hank, what
in hell were you doing knocking him out cold? Do you
really want to do jail time?"

"I didn't have much choice," the foreman said as
calmly as possible as he cradled his hand against his
chest. "He was going to arrest them for beating up Ken
Zane."

"Oh, so Zane was at the heart of this." Jo turned to
the other three men again. "He's the last man that you
boys should have gone near tonight."

"Well, we kinda felt that we should help Hank out," Jay defended himself. "He was getting the worst of it from Zane."

"What?" Back to Hank again, Jo was nearly beside herself with rage. "I expect you to baby-sit those fools and it turns out that you can't handle yourself. Are you...are you totally insane? No," she said, cutting off his rebuttal, "I don't want to know. Not another word."

Jo stalked back toward the bunkhouse where Dan was waiting patiently, leaning against the porch rail. Then she stopped, turning back to the men.

"You boys better be sober out there," she warned. "You better be awake and ready. If one drop of that poison touches Tate land, I swear I'm going to fire the lot of you. And I'll tell you something else, I've never made a threat that I didn't plan to back up. You had better watch it out there." Then, noticing Hank's swollen hand, she said, "What did you do to your hand? No, I don't want to know. Just tend to it and saddle up your horse. And saddle a horse for Andrew, too. He's coming along."

The men did as they were told without a word, moving with deliberate speed and being careful to show just how alert they were. Even David's post-fight euphoria wore off in the face of Jo's anger, because the last thing any of them wanted to do was to let Jo down.

"It looks like he broke something," Dan commented when Jo rejoined him on the porch.

"Good, I hope it hurts," she said sharply. Then she softened her tone, saying, "Maybe it would be a good idea if everybody here took a few lessons from you, Dan."

"Wouldn't hurt," he agreed. "I'd bet he did that damage to himself on the first punch. So, are you all set to fly?"

"I'm getting used to it," she allowed, resting her head on his shoulder as he slipped the warm support of his arm around her back.

"It grows on you."

"Yeah, like moss on a rock. Oh, here comes Andrew." She stepped away from him and down to the yard to await the sheriff's approaching vehicle.

A moment later, Andrew got out of the car and placed his Stetson firmly on his head. "You ought to get leashes for your boys, Jo," he said, approaching her. "Glen wants to form a posse to string them all up."

"He'll get over it in jail," Jo said. "Are we ready to go?"

"Just a second," Andrew said, then shouted at the men in the corral, "Hey, get your sorry butts over here! Now," he went on when they had gathered near by. "I'm going to deputize the bunch of you. Don't get any big ideas about what this means. All I'm doing is making our little excursion legal, not giving you free rein to bust anybody up out there. You got that?"

The crew nodded their understanding.

"Okay, raise your right hands," Andrew commanded. "You, too, Jo. I don't want anybody complaining that I brought civilians into trouble. Okay, do you all swear to uphold the law and promise not to screw up out there?"

"I do," came the unanimous reply.

"Good. You're all deputies. But only for tonight," he added, smiling. "Come sunrise, it evaporates like a magic spell. I'm not putting you on the payroll. Do you boys have any guns?"

"A couple rifles," Bill said. "A shotgun. Nothing very handy."

"Jo doesn't believe in shooting varmints," Hank explained, "so we mostly just chase coyotes away."

"It's probably best, anyway," Andrew said as he spun the cylinder of his own weapon. "You boys would probably end up shooting me. Bring the rifles along, just in case. I guess we're ready to go."

JO AND DAN HOVERED several hundred feet above the ground, the gravel pit on the Pettigrew ranch appearing as a slightly irregular, darkened patch below them in the mottled gray of the rangeland. They had been up there nearly an hour, but there was no sign below them yet, no light to show the passage of the truck along the road and south to where it might cross onto Tate land.

Dan was holding them virtually motionless in the sky, while they waited in silence for the most part. The noise from the engine kept them from engaging in small talk. However, they were secure in each other's presence, and could abide the lack of conversation without self-consciousness.

"They'll have to make their move soon," Jo said after a while. "If they get going in a hurry and get the truck stuck in a rut, they'll be sunk."

"Yeah, if they happened to think of that," Dan said. "But I agree, if only because they'll want to get it done and get to bed."

"I just wish they'd get on with it."

But there was still no sign from below, and all they could do was wait.

Jo took the night-vision binoculars in hand and trained them at the ground to search as meticulously as possible despite the slight swaying motion of the heli-

copter. A brief pinprick of light flared below them and
went out. That was probably Bill lighting a cigarette,
she decided. Other than that, there was no sign of life
for the next fifteen minutes.

When they had just about given up hope, their pa-
tience was rewarded. A pickup approached from the
south, following the narrow road to the north rapidly.
Jo watched anxiously as the fan of light bounced along
the rough road until they finally reached the point where
she and Dan had seen them hide the truck earlier. A
moment later, a second light snapped on and began
moving almost immediately to the south with the pickup
following behind.

"Turn on the camera," Dan said as he brought them
around to point the nose of the craft toward the moving truck.

Jo used the remote switch they had run in from outside through a small vent to activate the video camera.
Then she turned on the battery-operated television she
had borrowed from David. The screen fuzzed on and
then back to black, showing nothing at first. Jo grasped
a handle, which was connected to a mechanical control
like a universal joint. By turning and tilting this control, she was able to move the two arms on the front of
the helicopter that held four high-powered halogen
lamps—the helicopter's "headlights." It was to the right
one of these arms that they had affixed her video camera, using wire and duct tape for the most part. After a
moment of maneuvering, the small television screen
showed the headlights below them.

"I've got them," she said excitedly. "They're awfully dim."

"We'll light them up once they cross to your land."
Dan was maintaining their altitude, but he was now

flying on a course that kept them just behind the truck. "I hope the boys have seen it so they can start moving in."

"They must have, by now," Jo said, concentrating on keeping the camera trained on the vehicle below.

"Are you ready?" Dan spoke with clear concern then. "This isn't going to be a very smooth ride. You'll probably think roller coasters are tame stuff after we're finished here."

"I'm ready," she assured him. She only wished she felt as confident as she sounded. "Just don't run us into the ground."

"Okay, boss," he said, laughing. "I'll try hard not to."

Dan flipped down the night-vision visor on his helmet and tightened the strap beneath his chin. His palms were moist on the controls, but it wasn't from anxiety but excitement. The only thing he'd enjoyed about the army was flying, and his favorite flying was always the nighttime training exercises. He was in his element here.

"They're turning," Jo said, watching the screen as she double-checked her safety harness. "They're going right toward that creek bed like we thought they would."

"Just give the word," he said. "We'll drop on them like a bat out of hell."

"Wait one more minute. Wait a...no, what's that?" Jo tensed, seeing a flare of light from the front of the truck. There was another brief flare, and then an answering flash from the darkness beyond the headlights. "Oh, no, they're shooting at them. Now! Now, Dan! Hurry!"

Dan hit the switch for the high-beam lights and jammed the rudder forward. The helicopter responded instantly, diving as nearly vertically as possible while the entire craft shook and hummed in protest to the sudden stress of the dive.

At first, Jo could barely control the direction of the camera and lights, as her stomach rose into her throat and the G forces of the dive knocked her back into her seat. She found her free hand clutching her chair with knuckle-whitening pressure, her teeth gritted; but she had to concentrate on the task at hand, so she fought back the urge to scream in the face of her certain knowledge that they were going to smash into the ground below. Shifting her gaze quickly between the Plexiglas window before her and the small TV that was bouncing at her feet, she saw the ground expanding at an alarming rate of speed. The speck of white headlights grew and were then engulfed by the brighter glare of the helicopter's lights as the truck itself grew frightfully fast.

Dan kept them on course directly at the truck, while the man below them looked up in surprise, then raised his weapon toward the sky and began firing. Dan continued to dive into the bullets, swaying the craft from side to side to avoid becoming a steady target. Despite the evasive maneuver, one of the shots ricocheted off the side of the craft with a loud ping.

At fifty feet above the truck, he jerked the controls back, bringing them to the bottom of the roller coaster and up again at another sickening angle. Then, as the G forces held them back in their seats, he spun the helicopter on its tail and descended again, with Jo fighting to avoid blacking out from the dizzying force of their flight. He swooped over the truck at fifty miles an hour, turned and swooped again while the man tried ineffectively to hit them with bullets from below.

The crew of the Bar T had better luck, however. On their third pass, Dan could see one of the front tires of the truck explode from the impact of a rifle shot. The man from the truck began running then, dropping his weapon in his haste to get to the pickup that had been following behind.

"We're going after that pickup," Dan shouted. "Hang on!"

"Oh, it can't get any worse, can it?" Jo gritted her teeth and grasped the light control again. It wasn't as bad as the dive had been, but they were no more than fifteen feet above the ground, and the blur of motion in the lights was nearly as frightening.

The man caught the pickup in motion, throwing himself into the back as it was turning and bounding away from Tate land. Then they poured on the speed, flying over the ruts toward the road.

"Zoom the camera in," Dan shouted. "Get the license plate!"

"I've got it," Jo shouted back, keeping the camera trained on the truck that was rushing along the road just ahead of them.

"Good," Dan said. "This is the end of the road for us. Can't shoot them—can't land on them. Let's take her back."

"We did it, Dan!" she exclaimed. "We stopped them, and we've got evidence, too!"

"That was great!" Dan exclaimed exuberantly. "Hell of a ride, huh Jo?"

"Oh, yes," she said. "Just put us down on the ground fast."

Dan did as requested. Taking them smoothly back to where the men were standing by the truck, he deftly lowered the chopper to the ground. Jo had to admit, to herself, anyway, that after what she'd just been through, level flight was actually pleasant.

Hank ran up to the helicopter before they even touched ground, shouting and waving his hands. Dan cut the engine and threw open the canopy.

"What?" he called against the dying roar of the engine.

"Andrew," Hank replied. "He's been shot! Over here!"

With a cry of alarm, Jo threw herself from the craft and ran as best as she could on wobbling legs toward the other men. Andrew lay on the ground holding his stomach, a red stain growing ominously on the front of his shirt.

"Those boys had no manners," he said feebly, smiling up at her as she knelt beside him. "They didn't even let me show my badge."

"How is it?" she asked him. "Can you move?"

"Oh, sure, I'm just bleeding, is all. Strap me up on the horse and I'll get into town."

"You might make it a mile or so, but not much farther on horseback." Dan crouched beside the fallen man and tore open Andrew's shirt to reveal the dark puncture in the sheriff's stomach just above his navel. "Roll him over a bit," he told the men. When they did, he pulled the shirt quickly away from Andrew's back, as well.

"There's no exit wound," Dan said as he stood up again, wiping his bloodied hands on his pants. "We need to get him to a surgeon right away. Put something over the wound. The cellophane from a cigarette pack will work, and I've got some tape in the chopper. Flatten it out and tape it over the wound, then wrap it with something. We've got to get him to a hospital."

"We'll have to get a pickup out here," Hank said as he took off his shirt and began tearing it into strips for bandages.

"I'll fly him. Where's the nearest hospital with a trauma center? What direction from here?" Dan was already walking back toward the helicopter when he asked the question. "And how far is it?"

"It's in Great Falls," Jo called as she wrapped the strips of Hank's shirt over the plastic seal on the wound. "Nearly one hundred miles due west."

"Good," Dan called back. "I should have enough gas for that."

"He can't ride in a helicopter that far," she exclaimed.

"I've got that covered." Dan was busy in the front of his helicopter. Using a wrench from his tool kit, he quickly removed four bolts from the base of the front seat and then, unceremoniously, lifted it out of the craft and threw it aside. Then he pulled up a set of cargo straps from behind the pilot's seat and tied them to two sets of rings in the floor on either side of the cabin.

"Get him over here," he commanded. "We'll strap him in. Hurry! Jo, you'd better get the camera off the arm so we don't lose the tape."

Jo used Hank's knife to cut the makeshift binding off the camera, while the men carried the stricken law officer to the helicopter. Moments later they had maneuvered him inside, where he could almost stretch out on the floor.

"You're a bit taller than most cargo I carry, Sheriff," Dan commented as he packed horse blankets over him and tightened the straps on his chest and legs. "You'll have to bend your knees a bit. How you feeling?"

"Cold," Andrew said. "Kinda numb."

"Well, I hope to have you at the hospital in a little over an hour," Dan told him, pulling the portable TV out and handing it to one of the men beside him. "I don't suppose you know the radio frequencies for hospital traffic, do you?"

"Emergency network," Andrew said. "They can direct you."

"Good. You better stay conscious so you can help me contact them, all right, Sheriff? We'll be a team up there, okay? You have to stay awake."

"Yup," the man said stoically. "Tell those guys to keep an eye on the truck. They might be back. But stay out of it. Don't touch anything."

"We know what we're doing, Andrew," Hank said gruffly. "You just get back here fast, so you can take credit for the whole thing."

"Fly safely, Dan." Jo threw her arms around him as he turned from the helicopter, kissing him briefly before letting him go.

"I will. Lock your door tonight," he told her. "I hate leaving you alone like this. Maybe the men should stay up at the house tonight."

"Don't worry about me," she said. "I'll be fine."

There was no time for further assurances, because every second was important now, and Dan had to make the most of them. He kissed her again and then pulled himself up to his seat in the chopper.

"Stand clear!" He pulled the canopy shut and engaged the engine. A moment later he was gone on a race against the clock, leaving nothing but a swirling cloud of dust in his wake.

Jo watched his lights shrink in the distance with trepidation in her heart. They had kept the men from dumping the chemicals and had captured the truck, but Andrew was out of it, and the culprits had gotten away. It appeared to be a draw for now.

As she mounted the horse Andrew had ridden, she couldn't help but feel that the momentum had shifted away from them. As tight as the case seemed to be, she had the dreadful feeling that the perpetrators would find some way to wiggle out of it.

The videotape in her saddlebag was all they really had to convict them. She had to keep that tape safe at all costs. And that made her the next target.

Chapter Fifteen

"Great Falls control, this helicopter Delta Foxtrot Zero Niner Able. Come in, Great Falls control. Over." Dan keyed off the microphone and waited, listening to the static on his radio. There was no reply, so he adjusted the dial and tried again.

"Great Falls control, I have an emergency. I need routing to Methodist General Hospital. Over."

"Great Falls control. Come again. Over." The responding reply came through the hiss of static at last.

"Sunspots," Dan shouted at Andrew, glancing past his controls to where the lawman lay swaddled in blankets on the floor. "They really screw up reception." When the other man smiled wanly, he keyed on the microphone again.

"Great Falls control, this helicopter Delta Foxtrot Zero Niner Able," he repeated. "I have a medical emergency. Gunshot wound. I need routing to Methodist General Hospital. Over."

"I read you, Delta Foxtrot," the air controller replied, his voice stronger now. "What is your heading and ETA? Over."

"I am due east of your beacon. ETA thirty minutes. Over."

"Continue on course. We'll relay your information. Do you have any information on the nature of the injury? Over."

"Gunshot to the upper abdomen. Large-caliber rifle bullet. The patient is conscious and coherent. The bullet is still in him, but he seems all right so far. Over."

"Roger, Delta Foxtrot. Will relay and advise. Continue on course. Over."

"Roger. Over and out."

Dan checked the course on his electronic compass, flipped down his night visor for a brief look at the landscape ahead of them and then lifted it again to look down at Andrew.

"Less than half an hour now, Sheriff," he shouted.

Andrew said something but it wasn't audible over the sound of the helicopter.

"I'm sorry, Sheriff," Dan said. "I can't hear you. Don't shout, though. Too much strain. You just go ahead and talk all you want to keep awake. Okay?"

Andrew nodded, though his eyelids were drooping. Then he blinked his eyes open, shaking his head and saying something more.

"Don't worry about a thing," Dan said. "You just stay awake, and I'll avoid hitting any mountains. Deal?"

Andrew nodded.

Dan was flying about two hundred feet above the ground, following the terrain as it rose and fell, gaining altitude toward the higher peaks of the Rocky Mountains. He was passing over the northern reaches of the Big Snowy Mountains, an eastern branch of the Rockies to the southwest of the ranch. The terrain was definitely more rugged than it was around the Bar T Ranch.

Dan was keeping low to be certain of avoiding any commercial traffic as he followed his own unannounced flight path west. Flying low as he was, there was the danger of striking night birds, but it was preferable to have some doddering old Piper Cub suddenly pop up before him. As he flew, he wished he would have been a bit less stingy and paid the few extra dollars for the radar that had originally come with the helicopter. At the time, he had wanted to save money and flying weight and so had bought no more of the equipment than necessary.

But then, he hadn't expected to be ferrying a wounded man to a hospital in the dead of night, had he? No, yet here he was doing just that.

He glanced down at the sheriff on the floor. The man's eyes had slipped shut.

Dan couldn't shake him to attempt to rouse him, but he had to be certain that the man remained awake, so he shook the helicopter, instead. He bucked the chopper up and then violently down again to startle the man awake, and was rewarded by the sheriff's eyes instantly flying open.

"Don't fall asleep," Dan shouted, putting them back on an even course again. "Don't wimp out on me, Andy! Keep those eyes open for another twenty minutes, okay? Okay?" he asked more loudly.

Andrew nodded, blinking.

He was good for the effort, but Dan wasn't certain that his effort would be enough. Keeping a patient in shock awake until they could receive medical attention was the most important thing to do. If Andrew fell asleep, he might never regain consciousness.

Lord knows how much blood he's already lost internally, Dan thought. *I've got to fly faster.*

But he was already pushing the sleek craft to its limit. He could do no more than pray.

Faster!

"This is Jo Tate here, Gail. Do you read me?"

Jo rode along with Hank and David as they made their way slowly back to the ranch compound. Bill and Jay were staying with the truck for the evening, and the last she'd seen of them, they had been resolutely trying to raise a signal on David's portable television. It was an unusual sight, two cowboys sitting on their bedrolls in the midst of the dark plains watching the flickering screen of a five-inch television.

She had finally given in to her inner argument about calling the FBI agent now or waiting until morning when her enemies could be seen. She had finally decided that the men in the truck would never be found if she waited, so she picked up the microphone of the portable radio.

"Come on, Gail, this is Jo. Over."

"Hi, Jo." Gail Winston's voice came over the speaker. "What on earth are you doing up at this hour?"

"It's a long story. Can you get in touch with Agent Harden?" Jo asked.

"I suppose I can rouse him," the deputy said. "Why?"

"I don't know how much I can go into on the radio, Gail. Andrew has been injured." Now Jo regretted calling, because any explanation she gave would demand further explanation and still more beyond that. "He'll be fine. Dan is flying him to the hospital in Great Falls. I've got some evidence for Agent Harden."

"What's that got to do with Andy? Come on, Jo, what was he up to tonight?"

"I don't really have the details clear myself," Jo lied. "But he wanted Agent Harden to get on this as soon as possible. Could you have him call me?"

"I'll do that, Jo," Gail said. "Are you at home?"

"I will be," she replied. "I've got to go now. Over and out."

As she replaced the mike on the radio transmitter, she couldn't help but feel that she'd done something wrong in calling. Still, it couldn't be helped now.

GAIL SAT LOOKING at the radio for a full minute before rousing herself to turn her chair and reach for the telephone.

Glen entered just as she was about to dial, however, and she put the receiver down to speak to him.

"You're still up and about, too?" she asked. "What's gotten into everyone tonight?"

"What do you mean?" He grumbled at her and sat in the chair beyond the desk.

"Jo Tate just called. Do you know anything about what the sheriff was up to tonight?"

"I haven't seen him since he let Jo's boys leave town. It's obvious he has his own ideas about law enforcement these days, so I couldn't begin to guess."

"Stop being an idiot, Glen."

"Yeah, so what's with Jo tonight?"

"Something about Andrew. She said he was injured but didn't say what happened. I'm worried, Glen."

"If it was serious, she would have told you, wouldn't she?" Glen slipped to the front edge of his chair, his gaze sharpening as he spoke. "Where is Andrew?"

"Dan Fitzpatrick is flying him to the hospital in Great Falls. She wanted me to wake up Agent Harden and have him call her, too. It's something about evidence. I don't know, we should have been informed if Andrew was doing something tonight. I don't like this one bit."

"Evidence?" Glen mused quietly. "Of what?" He sat a moment tapping one knuckle against his lips. Then he stood suddenly. "I don't like it, either," he said. "I think Harden is out of town tonight, though. Maybe he was in on whatever happened. Hell, it's probably all some FBI thing and they were too uppity to let us in on it."

"Don't you go out to the ranch, though," Gail warned him. "Remember what the sheriff said about mixing it up with the Bar T boys."

"Yes, I remember," Glen said as he walked through the door. "I sure don't plan to talk to any of those boys."

"IT'S JUST PLAIN STUPID to worry about them now," Jo had said to Hank and David when the two men insisted on following her to the main house. "They're probably in Canada by now."

"Maybe, but I'd like to take a look around just to make certain," Hank said as they entered the house. "I know you're the boss and all, but I think I'll have to forget that for a minute or two."

He and David had gone from one room to the next until they were certain that there was no one hiding in the house and that every window was securely locked. Only then had they begun to relax a bit and admit that it didn't make much sense for the dumpers to have run here after their brief skirmish.

Still, Hank had elected to sleep on the porch for the remainder of the evening, while he ordered David to take a position on the living-room couch.

Jo chided them for their worries, but in the end was grateful for the concern they showed. And now, lying in her bed with the videotape at arm's reach on her bedside table, she tried to find the sleep she so desperately craved. She was glad they hadn't listened to her protests. In the morning, after an uneventful night, they could laugh about it. For now, however, she felt much safer being under guard.

But what about Dan and Andrew? It was her concern for them that was keeping her awake now, and there was no way for her to guard against that worry.

Dan was surely a competent pilot, so she wasn't concerned about his flying. But it was possible he might have misjudged the amount of fuel left in the helicopter, and the image of the craft slipping silently out of the air to crash into suburban Great Falls haunted her each time she closed her eyes.

And what about Andrew? He had been her friend for as long as she could remember. All she could see now was his stoic smile and the blood that covered his stomach. It was a long flight to the hospital. What if they arrived too late?

It was her fault that he was involved, after all. She should have told the FBI agents everything from the start and been done with it. Only her own stubbornness had kept her from voicing her suspicions in her own defense. What was it about her that made her value her independence above everything else—even, it seemed, the truth?

Well, she'd done right on that score by calling for the agent now. Now, if he would ever call her back, he

could put out a warrant on the pickup truck and appre-
hend the polluters. Yes, calling him was the best thing
she could have done. And now that they had concrete
evidence and official confirmation of what had taken
place, she could see the end of the investigation fast
approaching. They would lift the restrictions on her
herd and release her accounts once more, and she would
be free to spend the rest of her life with Daniel, which,
she was pretty sure, was what he had in mind, too.

Mrs. Daniel Fitzpatrick.

No, Jo Tate Fitzpatrick? Just Jo Tate? She couldn't
decide.

Jo smiled at her indecision. Of course, if they were to
get married, she would keep the Tate name, there was
no question about that. How she would keep it was the
question. After all, the only thing she had against the
name Fitzpatrick was the fact that Tate was the name on
the gate to the ranch. She loved him and wanted to be
with him always, but she sure wasn't going to change
the brand for him. No, she wouldn't go against history.

And he would understand. He was a Texan, after all.

A Texan. She should have known that she'd have to
import a man if she ever wanted to find true love.
Again, she smiled, thinking of how she had begun to
think that she would never find love. But she had found
it, or rather, it had found her. Now that she had love,
she couldn't clearly remember what life had been like
without it.

The wonderful, luxurious thought of love allowed her
mind to relax at last. She lay with the image of Dan's
face in her mind, while his laughter rang happily
through her ears. The thoughts of him were such a
powerful presence that she could almost feel the silken
skin of his back beneath her hands as she remembered

their shower, the hot water, their lovemaking. She fel
a yearning more powerful than she'd ever known be
fore. Now that she had a face, a body, upon which t
focus her inner needs, the desires that had long seeme
dormant came to the fore with a force that made he
sigh. But they weren't the anxious, dizzying desires o
a young girl with no expectation of love. No, this wa
the softly sensual desire of a woman who knew tha
everything she wanted would be hers soon.

She had already held what she wanted, and soon sh
would have the chance to explore the new territory o
her lover's body. Soon, the warm desires that lulled he
now would be more than mere desire. They would b
memories, and they would be hers alone.

Then sleep crept in over her, pulling her eyelids dow
to shut out the dim moonlight and the shadow tha
moved briefly across her window.

HANK STIRRED on the porch. He had purposely chose
to spread his sleeping bag out on the wooden glider an
lie on top of it rather than seek a more comfortabl
berth. His hand hurt like blazes, anyway—the little
finger swollen to twice its normal size—so a little more
discomfort wouldn't harm him. He didn't want to sleep
soundly, though he realized that sleep was inevitabl
after the night he'd already put in.

He had put David inside behind the locked door as a
second line of defense. David was a much sounde
sleeper than he was, anyway, and so wouldn't have been
much good on the porch. Besides, he was just a kid—a
big, affable kid—and Hank worried about him. No
that he would ever admit to such a worry, of course. I
just wasn't in his nature to cut the kid any slack.

Hank fell asleep quickly, considering the throbbing pain of his hand, and he lay on the gently swaying glider with his booted feet up over one arm and his head jammed against the other, both arms folded across his chest. The occasional movements of the horses in the corral caused him to stir slightly, for even in sleep he was on guard.

He wasn't sure what woke him, but he came awake suddenly and completely and lay very still listening for a sound to tell him what was wrong. There was nothing. But something had awakened him, and it wasn't the horses.

There! A small click at the other end of the porch. That was it!

He rolled off the glider and to his feet in one easy motion, gritting his teeth against the sudden blast of pain from his hand, and snatched the rifle he had leaned against the wall beside him. Walking quickly, he crossed to the end of the porch and swung the gun around the corner, leaning past the rail.

There was nothing there.

He waited a moment and then drew back from the rail, hearing the slight creak of dry wood too late. As he turned back quickly, the club struck Hank on the side of the head before he could even see who was there. He was unconscious before he hit the porch.

The redheaded man smiled as he turned and walked back to the door in his stocking feet. He tried the knob lightly, but it was locked, so he motioned to the other man who had come around the front of the house after he had subdued the ranch foreman.

Ken Zane crept up to the porch by the burly redhead. He held the man's boots in one hand, and he gave

them to him and then knelt at the door and bega
working at it with his lock picks.

A moment later, they had the door unlocked and en
tered the house with the same quiet sureness they ha
displayed outside. David stirred as they entered, givin
away his position in the dark room by the slight huff
ing sound he made as he came awake. They made sur
that he didn't wake enough to identify them, and the
laid him down on the couch once more.

"Quiet now," Ken whispered. "I think I know whic
room is hers."

Beyond the barrier of her bedroom door, Jo stirre
slightly as sounds of movement in the house slippe
through to her. For the moment, she slept on, conten
to continue dreaming of love.

"WAKE UP, Andrew! Come on, we're here! Wake up!"
Dan leaned over the unconscious law officer, shoutin
at him as he untied the straps that had secured him t
the helicopter floor. "Come on, we made it!" h
shouted once more, as the hospital staff reached him.

"Out of the way, buddy," an orderly commanded
"We'll get him."

Dan complied, standing well back of the white-cla
medical workers who clambered onto the chopper. The
pulled Andrew up from inside and lowered him to th
hospital gurney. They had him wheeled away from th
heliport in seconds, leaving Dan feeling somewha
numb beside the helicopter.

"I haven't seen one of these since Vietnam," a
woman said behind him.

"What?" Dan turned, startled to see a middle-age
woman in white smiling up at him. "Oh, sorry, yo
startled me."

"That's all right. You look dead tired, son," the woman told him. "You're going to have to answer a few questions for us, but then I think we can fix you up with someplace to sleep."

"That sounds real nice," Dan said as he walked beside her toward the hospital. "I'm not used to flying medevac."

"Well, you got him here alive, so I guess you did all right."

"What about my helicopter," Dan asked. "Will it be all right there?"

"We have plenty of room if anyone else comes in," she assured him. "Come on now. We'll get the paperwork out of the way so you can catch a couple hours' sleep."

Dan thought about calling Jo to tell her he'd arrived safely, but once the papers were filled out, and he'd finally gotten a chance to talk to someone about Andrew's condition, it was too late to bother her. He didn't have any answers for her, and she needed her sleep, too. Besides, there would be time to talk tomorrow.

JO AWOKE with a start when someone closed the door to the bedroom next to hers. It was only the barest tap of wood on wood, but it woke her because it didn't fit in with the rest of the household sounds. The sound of a footstep in the hall got her out of bed. She stepped quietly into her jeans and slipped her blouse on while she toed one foot around on the floor trying to locate her boots in the dark.

It might be Hank checking things out, but she didn't really think so. And, if it wasn't Hank or David, it would definitely not be a good idea to open the bedroom door.

She found her boots and picked them up, clutching them awkwardly, along with the videotape, as she backed toward the window, hoping she could get it open without making noise. But the bedroom door opened swiftly, and a dark figure outlined against the darker hall stepped in. And then the beam of a flashlight snapped on and washed over her rumpled bed, the dresser and wall, and finally came to rest on her as she cocked her arm back and threw both boots at the man with the flashlight.

He grunted in pain, dropping the light, but there was another man with him and he rushed her, grabbing her and pinning her on her stomach to the bed.

"What's this?" the man hissed in her ear as he pushed her arm up behind her back and pulled the videotape from her fingers. She didn't recognize his voice, but she did recognize the next man who spoke.

"Do we have a little videotape bonus here?" Ken Zane said. "Is that what you were doing in the chopper? A bit of aerial reconnaissance, was it?"

"Take a flying leap, Zane," she shouted against the bed. "You're not getting away with any of this."

"Of course we are," he said. Then he grasped the back of her head and turned her face into the pillow, pressing her down hard. "We've got you and your evidence."

Jo fought against the men, but the two of them were just too much for her, and the smothering effect of the pillow began to sap her strength until she could fight no more. After two minutes, it was all she could do to remain conscious, and she lay as limp as a rag doll.

"Okay." Zane released his grip, letting her breathe. "Now that you're nice and quiet, we're going to take a little trip."

Jo felt defeated, beaten. But she hadn't the strength to fight them. It was no use risking her life in a futile attempt to protect the videocassette.

Suddenly, her sheet was thrown over her and she was rolled in it, wrapped as tightly as a moth in its cocoon. Then she was lifted, writhing against the constricting fabric, and carried out of her house and into the night, as the horses in the corral cried out in response to her own muffled cries.

Two minutes later, however, all was silent again.

Chapter Sixteen

Dan sat up on the waiting-room couch, where he had spent the night, and got slowly to his feet. He still felt dog tired, but he wouldn't be able to walk if he spent any more time curled up on the couch. The doctor had offered him a vacant bed, but he had refused her, thinking it would be better if he didn't get too comfortable. He had to get back to the ranch, after all, and hadn't wanted to oversleep.

Now he stretched his arms up over his head, painfully working the kinks out, and pulled his fingers through his hair in an effort to comb it. Rubbing one hand over the stubble on his jaw, he went in search of a bathroom where he could attempt to make himself presentable.

A quick splash of cold water was the best he could do, but at least he no longer looked as though he'd just gotten up. Next, he found the front desk and inquired about the sheriff's condition.

"He's sleeping now," the nurse told him, consulting a chart before her. "Surgery went well, apparently. His condition is listed as guarded."

"What does that mean?"

"He'll be all right, but we have to keep an eye on him," she explained, smiling.

"Do you have any idea when he might be awake?"

"I can't say for sure, but I expect it would be some-time this afternoon."

"Okay, thank you."

Dan found a pay phone and dialed the ranch num-ber. There wasn't anything more for him to do here, but Jo might want him to stay until he knew more about Andrew's condition. The phone rang six times on the other end before someone picked it up.

"Yeah?"

"Hank? This is Dan. Is Jo handy? I want to talk to her."

"Oh, no, she's—" Hank said hesitantly. "Get your ass back here, flyboy, Jo's missing."

"What! Dammit, Hank, what were you guys doing back there!"

"Don't shout, my head's about to burst as it is," Hank said miserably. "Just get back here as fast as you can."

"Okay, okay, I'm on my way," Dan said quickly. "Oh, Andrew is going to be all right," he added just before hanging up.

"When Sheriff Hollander wakes up, tell him Dan had to fly back," he told the nurse at the desk. "I'll call his folks, and all that. Tell him not to worry."

Dan rushed away from the desk with no further word of explanation. He had to gas up his bird and get out of there—quickly.

If Jo is harmed in any way, I'll kill the bunch of them, he vowed. And Daniel Fitzpatrick had never gone back on a promise.

"ADDING KIDNAPPING to the charges they've already got piled up against you isn't very intelligent. You're only making it worse!" Jo lay rigidly on the floor where the men had thrown her, the sheet still securing her body so that she was unable to move other than to roll slightly.

Enough light filtered through the cotton to tell her that it was well into morning, but she couldn't see any of the men whom she could hear walking on the echoing floorboards of the line shack. The day's heat had already grown to the point where she was roasting in her cocoon, and the air she breathed was hot and stale.

"The best thing you can do is run while you have the chance," she said as calmly as possible. "You're just digging a deeper hole."

"Shut up, woman!" the man she hadn't recognized barked at her, the sound of a chair scraping the floor accompanying his words.

"No, you shut up," Zane spoke quietly, a commanding whisper iced with contempt. "And put that gun away."

"She keeps on talking—" the man began, but he stopped quickly, as though afraid of Zane. "Hell, you're crazy," he said to some threat that Jo couldn't see.

"Just put the gun away and be quiet. Hell, she ain't going to rush you like that, is she?"

Jo heard footsteps approaching her, and then a hand patted her shoulder and smoothed slowly down the taut fabric over her chest. "So you think we're digging a hole?" Zane asked her. "I think we're climbing out of one."

"You're adding years to your sentence once you're caught."

"Are they going to catch us?" His hand continued to stroke lightly over her body as he spoke.

"If you stick around here, they are," she said. His touch made her feel dirty, violated, even through the layers of wrapped cloth.

"We have to hear about the sheriff's condition first." Zane laughed. "If he dies, then we know what to do with you."

"And if he lives?"

"Then there's no point in killing you," he replied easily. "That makes sense, doesn't it?"

"My boys still know what's going on," she said stubbornly.

"But they're not credible witnesses. No, we can definitely make them into liars if they try spouting anything. If the sheriff lives, of course, then there's nothing we can do but cut our losses and run."

"You don't plan to stick around here in either case, do you?"

"The people I work for now have title to Pettigrew's ranch," Zane explained. "Do you think we really want to walk away from prime land like that? No, I'd rather take a little heat to hang on to our investment."

"So you killed him to get his ranch?"

"Not directly," Zane admitted. "He had an attack of conscience. You know, I didn't think he had one until then." He pressed his hand against her breast once more, then removed it.

Jo was silent. The effort to talk while breathing this stale air was too much for her and she had to rest.

It did make sense, though. When Pettigrew had overextended himself buying cattle a few years back, everyone thought he had worked his way out of the bind through better management. Now it was apparent that

that hadn't been the case, and that, instead, he'd probably borrowed the money against the promise of giving these men a place to make their illegal dumps. When it became apparent what he had promised for the money, he'd probably flown into one of his typical rages and threatened his new creditors. Unfortunately, this time his threats were against men who used lethal means to settle their disputes. She could almost feel sorry for him. Almost.

"What about the cattle?" Jo asked then.

"That's what set the old guy off," Zane said. "They wandered into some bad grass. We moved them to your ranch, but he figured out what killed them after talking to you on the phone."

"And my cattle?"

"We fed them some of the same grass," Zane laughed. "It wouldn't do to have your cattle unaffected if we were going to blame you for everything."

"You're a sorry bastard," Jo hissed. "I feel sorry for Mary."

"Mary is too easy. She pines over that ignorant foreman of yours, yet comes back to me when he won't do anything to get her back. I guess some women never learn when to stop playing hard to get."

She heard him stand then, walking away, and heard the low whispering of two men talking. Footsteps again, and Zane's hand patted her hip.

"We're going out for a while," he said. "Don't worry, we'll be back. Oh, and I took the liberty of wrapping some tape around you so that the sheet won't work free. You can save your energy and not bother trying to wiggle out of it."

"Uncover my face at least," she asked. "I can barely breathe."

"Barely is good enough for me," he said. "I'll be back soon."

She heard both sets of boots walking across the floor and, a moment later, the sound of a car starting and driving away. Then there was silence, except for the occasional chirping of a bird.

Was she still guarded? She had no way of knowing, but she had to try to free herself, in any case. When she struggled against her binding, she realizing it wasn't very likely that she would get free. Her only hope now was with Dan.

DAN'S HELICOPTER hurled across the sky toward the east with the lean young pilot straining forward in his seat, anxiously watching every inch of territory that flew by below him. No matter how fast the blur of grass went past, it wasn't fast enough for him just then. Even more than last night, it was deathly important that he make good time.

I'm going to get back, find them and kill them, he told himself. *It's as easy as that. No one harms Jo while I'm around to stop it. Nobody at all.*

He knew full well what had prompted both Hank and Andrew to say similar words to him. The woman was honest, straightforward, courageous, beautiful and humorous—really too good to be true—and no man could help but love her once he knew her. The fact that she had chosen him over the other suitors in her life gave him a sense of awe, as though a deity had plucked at his sleeve to select him from among all mortal men to receive immortality. He certainly didn't see himself as being in any way better than Andrew, yet she'd chosen him over the stalwart lawman.

Now he might lose her because some fool couldn't accept defeat gracefully and run while he had the chance. Some fool was looking to die, and Dan was in no mood to disappoint him.

Several times en route he had picked up the microphone to call ahead but had replaced it almost immediately. As much as he wanted to know if there had been any further developments, he wanted even more to arrive without announcing it to everyone. There were too many ears on the plains.

He was left to watch the miles roll by while the roar of the engine continued driving through his brain like a piston pounding home the urgency of his flight. He had to think, to plan ahead, but he could do neither while the thought of Jo's being in jeopardy filled his head. He needed to figure out what he would do when he finally got there, but for now he didn't have a clue.

"HELLO? Is anybody here?"

Jo rocked herself slightly, continuing until she was able to roll over and away from the wall. She was stopped almost immediately by the leg of a chair or table.

"Come on, who's here?" she said angrily. "You could at least let me use the outhouse! You people are inhuman!"

After a moment, she heard boots walking across the floor toward her. Then she heard a small click and there was a feeling of tugging at the fabric that held her.

"Hello?" she asked again, but there was no reply. Instead, someone pushed her and she rolled back toward the wall and out of the sheet.

The air in the cabin felt wonderfully cool after what she'd been breathing for the last several hours, and she lay a minute just enjoying the feeling as a slight breeze began to dry the perspiration from her skin. Then she rolled to her back and sat up stiffly to look up at her benefactor.

"Are you all right?" Glen asked as he closed the knife he had used to cut the tape that confined her. "Can you walk?"

"I probably can," she admitted, watching him. "Why are you mixed up in all this, Glen?"

"Me?" He pushed his hat back on his head as he stood and stared down at her in surprise. "Christ, Jo, what do you take me for?"

"Ken Zane is your buddy, isn't he? I just assumed you were in on it."

"You really don't like me much, do you?" he said sourly. "Just because I had a few laughs with the guy doesn't make us partners in crime."

"No, I suppose it doesn't. I just . . . well, I'm sorry."

"That's fine, Jo. Let's just get you out of here now."

"How did you figure out to look here?"

"Just a hunch," the deputy said, turning toward the door. "Agent Harden was out of town when you called for him. I've been checking around since then. We'd better hurry now. Damn!"

"What?"

"Someone is coming," he said simply.

DESPITE HIS ANXIOUS NEED for speed, Dan brought the helicopter in to the ranch on an evasive course that took him far to the north. He didn't want to be seen on arrival. He'd rather get to the ranch and have Hank fill him in on what happened before anyone knew he was back.

His route was taking him over the northern portion of Pettigrew property, so he took the helicopter to a thousand feet to avoid detection from the ground. Even from that height, however, he could discern the passage of a vehicle going north below him. It had to be going to the north line shack, where they had seen the truck parked the other night.

Yes, that must be where they were keeping her!

He nearly gave in to the urge to dive at the shack right then, but knew full well that he couldn't save her alone. Still, she was so close! How he wished the helicopter was still equipped with cannons and .50-caliber machine guns. He was loath to continue on and leave her there, but as he passed over the dark, dusty mass of the Pettigrew herd, he began to formulate a plan of action.

Dan turned toward the ranch again, making a broad curve east and south until the Bar T was in view. Once there, he dropped quickly toward the compound, which was alive with the motion of men and vehicles. He landed behind the bunkhouse near the fuel tank, leaped from the craft and ran to the ranch yard toward where Hank was standing with Agent Harden.

"What happened?" he asked breathlessly as he stopped at their side. "What happened to Jo?"

"It's all my fault," Hank said. He was barely recognizable behind a heavy bandage that covered the side of his face. The purplish mass of swollen flesh exposed at the edges of the bandage spoke of a near deadly blow, and each movement he made seemed to cause him great pain. "I figured it would be best to put me on the porch and David inside. I guess I should've had us both outside. It was a foolish mistake."

"But how did it happen?"

"They snuck up on them," Harden said to Dan. "We don't know who or how many people there were, but Jo Tate is gone as well as the videotape that I've been told you obtained last night. Our doctor says that the injuries the men received are consistent with those a police baton might make."

"Glen Wright," Dan said angrily.

"Yeah, I'd say so," Hank agreed.

"When did they get her?"

"We don't know," the agent said. "Early this morning, Jo called the sheriff's office requesting that I be awakened to contact her. I was out of town."

"He woke his friends, instead," Hank said.

"We have no idea why they took Miss Tate," Agent Harden said. "There is no benefit to them in committing a kidnapping. All they're doing is making things worse for themselves. I've called for a hostage-response team to meet us here, and we'll be ready to move as soon as we can figure out where they are keeping her."

"I know that already," Dan said. "She has to be in the same north line shack where we saw the tanker truck parked the other day. I saw a car headed that direction on my way back here."

"If that's the case, I can have it surrounded within an hour," Harden said.

"No," Dan advised him. "You don't want to create a hostage situation if you can avoid it. I've got a better idea."

"I can't authorize action without proper force to back it up, Fitzpatrick," he replied. "No matter what you may think, we can't take any unwarranted risks."

"You don't need to risk anything at all," Dan said. "I need a helicopter pilot, though. You have a pilot on your crew. What's his name—Grimes?"

"Yes, he's our pilot, but I don't see where—"

"I need a diversion," Dan interjected. "If I have to get her by myself, I will, but you can make it a whole lot easier."

"I'm not letting you out of here to endanger yourself and Miss Tate!"

"You aren't stopping me, either," Dan said forcefully. "Jay!" he shouted at the wrangler just stepping down from the porch. "Can you fuel up the helicopter? I've got to get some things together, and I want to be ready to take off right away."

"Will do," the man shouted back as he began to run toward the craft behind the bunkhouse.

"You can't go—"

"I am going," Dan insisted. "It would work out better if you let me use your pilot, but I'm going in either case."

"All right," Harden said after a thoughtful pause. "Grimes," he called to the man leaning against a gray sedan. "You go ahead with this fool, and we'll see what kind of plan he's got."

"Right, sir," the agent responded.

"Thank you," Dan said curtly. Then, to Hank, he said, "Can you ride?"

"If I have to," the man said, setting his jaw.

"I need you boys to get up to Pettigrew's herd as fast as possible. It's about five miles this side of that line shack with a crew working them. I bet they'll help if you lay it out for them. I'll give you half an hour head start."

"Sure, we can probably make it. Why?"

"I need you to start a little stampede," Dan said, smiling. "Just run those cows at the shack. That's all."

The smile that spread across Hank's face showed that the man felt the task was worth the headache.

"YOU HAD BETTER get out of here," Glen said to Jo. He removed the gun from his holster and checked the cylinder, then snapped it shut and reholstered it. "They'll be here in a couple minutes."

"What are you going to do?"

"My duty, I guess," he said grimly. "I don't suppose they'll cotton to being arrested, but I'll give it a try."

"You'd better take cover with me. Don't try anything foolhardy."

"No." He was watching out the door as he spoke, and now he took a step back toward her. "Get out back, out of the line of fire. Don't do anything stupid like trying to run for it. There's no cover for miles, so you'll never make it. Hurry up. They're coming."

Jo allowed herself to be propelled out the front door and then ran around to the back of the shed and hunched down near the wall. A moment later, the pickup skidded to a halt in front of the shack, and she heard the men get out.

"What's up, Glen?" Zane's demanding tone came clearly through the wall of the shack.

"You can probably guess," Glen told him.

"Probably," Ken replied. "Are you going to read me my rights?"

"You know your rights. Just put your hands up and keep quiet."

The next thing she heard was a gunshot.

Chapter Seventeen

"Take me in high and from the north. I'll jump well away from the shack." Dan was in the bunkhouse, hunched over a map of the area with agents Grimes and Harden, and was pointing out the location of the line shack on Pettigrew's property. He had changed into a pair of old green fatigue pants and a camouflage jacket over a T-shirt, and was busy forcing a twelve-inch nunchaku into one of the long pockets of the pants as he spoke.

"It's a long shot," Harden said gruffly. "Especially if you aren't taking any better weapon than two sticks of wood."

"Have you ever been hit by one of these?" Dan asked.

Dan withdrew the weapon from his pocket. The martial arts weapon, made up of two twelve-inch sticks of oak joined by a short length of stainless steel chain, was Dan's only backup to his bodily skill. A skilled person could swing a nunchaku around and around, from hand to hand, so fast that it became a blur of motion, a deadly blur that might strike out at any moment. Dan didn't claim any such proficiency, but he could use them well enough to get the job done. Anyone who had ever been struck by a nunchaku knew just what a lethal job it could do.

"No," the agent said. "Of course I've never been struck with those chopsticks, or whatever they're called. But I know they won't replace a .44 Magnum."

"No, they won't. But nunchaku are deadly enough to be illegal in some states," Dan explained.

He held one stick, spun the other around in a blur before him and then snapped it down on the top of the table with a resounding *thwack*. The wooden tabletop showed a definite impression and had splintered slightly where it had been struck.

"It makes a much stronger statement than a police baton," Dan said. "And from a greater distance."

"If you get that close," Harden said. "This plan is pretty loose."

"Should work, though," Grimes added, nodding toward the map. "The wind is in his favor for the jump. It looks like a long flight out there, though. Are you sure you can hang on?"

"I'll hang on, don't worry about that."

"So you're proposing to fly out there hanging on to the strut of the helicopter?" Harden stood up and smoothed the creases in his slacks. "All so you can parachute in on them? Are you an idiot?"

"I can't open the canopy and get out against the pressure of the rotor blades," Dan explained. "I've tied a length of rope onto the landing strut to hang on to. Besides, I'll be wearing a parachute, so falling off won't be any worse than jumping."

"Why not just land the darn thing?"

"We'd have to land miles away to avoid their hearing us. I can drop in fairly close."

Agent Harden looked at the map and then at Dan again. Finally, he shook his head and shrugged.

"Okay, I'll sign off on it," he said. "It's your neck, after all, but my team will be coming in right behind the cattle. If you don't get her out, we're coming in."

Harden walked out of the building, leaving Dan and the younger agent alone. "I haven't flown a Cobra in about ten years," Grimes said. "You sure you want me taking her up?"

"You're all I've got," Dan said, grinning. "Besides, if you crash it, you'll be the one in it when it goes down, not me. Now, after I'm down, I want you to wait until I'm in position and then come in low and fast on a strafing run. I want you in so low that you leave a groove in the roof on your way past. You got that?"

"I've got it. Are you sure you don't want a gun?"

"No. Just between you and me, I'm a lousy shot." Dan checked his watch. "Well, the men should be working on the Pettigrew herd by now. We'd better get moving so they don't get there ahead of us."

Jo FROZE beside the building, waiting for a noise or anything to tell her what had happened in the shack. She feared the worst, however, because there was only one gunshot and nothing after that. If Glen had shot one of them and subdued the other, or merely fired to scare them, she would have heard voices after the shot. Instead, there had been nothing.

Nothing, until there was a slight scuffling sound behind her and a hand grasped her shoulder, pulling her up and against the wall of the shack.

"Out sightseeing?" Zane thrust his grinning face close to hers, staring coldly into her eyes. "Or were you waiting to see who got shot?"

"I was rather hoping it was you," she replied. She could bring her knee up hard into his groin and possibly get away right then, but there was still another man to contend with, and neither of them would hesitate to shoot her if they had to.

"Sorry. I hate to disappoint you, but I was just a bit faster on the draw." He laughed, shaking her roughly against the weathered wood. "Now get in there."

He shoved her to the side, and she fell to her knees in the dirt. Laughing, he prodded her with the toe of his boot to move her along more quickly. The redheaded man was waiting at the table, idly turning an empty shell casing over between his fingers and looking down at the revolver on the table before him.

"Sit," Zane commanded.

Jo took a place across from the redheaded man, avoiding his gaze only to have her eyes fall upon the deputy's body lying face to the wall. She tried to look away but couldn't. A moment ago he had been alive, and now he was dead. It was as simple as that.

"Poor old Glen had trouble keeping an eye on two men at once," Zane said. "He was probably still hungover."

"You scum."

"Whatever you say." Ken shrugged. "But I'm rich scum."

"Money won't matter in jail. They'll be here for you soon."

"They don't know where we are," the burly redhead put in. "But we should get out of here."

"We will." Zane kept his eyes on Jo as he spoke, moving them predatorily over her face, which was framed by the tendrils of hair left limp by her confinement. "It looks like our friend the sheriff is going to make it," he said, still watching.

"Good," she said simply, returning his stare vehemently. "How do you know?"

"We went down to the ranch and called," he said. "The accountants are there trying to figure out if there's any money left. Our accountants, I should say."

"Your people really put their hooks into poor old Norton, didn't they? And now you've sent your number crunchers in to finish the job."

"A man's got to make a buck," he said. "Besides, Norton Pettigrew was an ornery fool who didn't have a friend left on earth, anyway. He called us for the loan, you know."

"And you were happy to oblige," she snapped. "You really don't care, do you? How many other places have you despoiled, Zane? Do any of the companies you haul for know what you're doing?"

"I'm not in customer relations," he said. "I don't care who knows what about anything. And, no, I don't much care where this stuff goes. I'm paid well for my efforts, and I'll get to retire soon and enjoy myself. That's what I care about. In fact, it's all I care about."

"I hope you get a chance to retire real soon," Jo said. "You'll get a lifetime of rest and relaxation at the state's expense for all of this."

"Yeah, and I'll burn in hell, too." Zane laughed, throwing his head back in raucous merriment. "Well, it's been fun chatting with you," he said after a moment. "But we really must be getting along."

"And you'll leave me lying beside Glen when you go," she said.

"Don't be so eager to die," he said. "You're coming along with us for a while."

"Oh, goody, a reprieve."

"A man's got to have insurance these days," Zane said. "I figure that you're a pretty good, paid-up policy. And I've been thinking that I might not have to kill you."

"I'd appreciate it," she said sarcastically.

"You're a good-looking woman, Jo. If you were nice to us, we might cut you some slack," he suggested, stepping closer to her. "I'll bet you could be nice if you tried."

"Not that nice. I'd rather die," she retorted vehemently. "Besides, it's just a lie, anyway."

"Not necessarily. There's enough evidence against you to make it pretty hot for you. This kidnapping could look like a slight falling-out with your partners."

"What evidence? That lame note you left in my office?"

"I planted evidence in your computer the other night, too. It implicates you right from the start of it all."

"How?"

"Those accountants the FBI are relying on to sort through Pettigrew's books are actually there to clean up the accounts. They just toted up everything in a separate account on a computer disk, and I transferred the works to your hard disk before I went to put the gun back. I put it in a separate directory, away from the rest of your bookkeeping, but they'll find it soon enough. It's all true," he added. "Except the one receiving the payments was Pettigrew, not you. And of course, the people paying him were different from what your file says."

"You thought of everything, didn't you?"

"I tried."

"And that's why you'll have to kill me, no matter what you say. You can't have me around to dispute the file."

"I suppose not," he admitted with a sigh. "When Pettigrew's silent partners step forward to claim the ranch, we want everything free and clear."

"Nothing is free and clear," she said.

"Maybe not." He picked up the videotape from the top of a weathered washstand, opened the front flap and began pulling the tape out of the case. "And we're not clear yet, either. Maybe they're just over the ridge waiting for us to make a move. I'd look pretty stupid coming out of here with just my old buddy Shorty here at my side," he said, pointing at the grinning redhead. "Can't hardly use him as a hostage. Hell, he's too good a target."

"See? I couldn't even trust your word to a lady, could I?" she said.

"No, ma'am," he said. "But it's not that far to the border. You won't have to wait long. Tie her up, Shorty. Just her hands. I don't want to have to carry her."

Shorty grabbed a short length of rope that was looped over the back of his chair and extended it toward her.

Jo hesitated at first, but there was, obviously no point in refusing him except to buy a few minutes of time. She didn't expect, however, that enough time could ever be bought to purchase rescue from these men. She had even begun to despair of Dan arriving to help her, though she knew that if he could find her, there would be nothing on earth that would stop him.

Zane continued idly pulling tape from the cassette as Shorty worked, unreeling all of their work in a few minutes until it lay in a pile of shimmering brown tape at his feet. When he had it all out, he dropped the now-empty case on top of the pile and took a book of matches from his pocket.

"I don't know how you think it will help to destroy the tape," Jo said, wincing slightly at the tightness of the rope around her wrists. "There are too many witnesses now."

"Not many witnesses to my face," he said. "Not many witnesses to the license of my pickup. No, I'm going to kill that witness right now."

He grabbed a yellowed, old newspaper from the top of the washstand and rolled it into a tube. Then he struck a match and set fire to the end of it, the dry paper catching quickly and leaping into flame. Zane stooped and thrust the burning paper into the pile of videotape, melting and shriveling the looped plastic as a foul, acrid smoke rose to fill the cabin.

When he was satisfied, he stood and waved at the smoke around his head.

"Fire up the truck, Shorty," he commanded. "It's time to hit the trail." Then he bowed slightly toward Jo. "Ladies first."

"What a gentleman," she scoffed.

But a surprised cry from the redhead at the door interrupted their conversation, and they both turned to look at him.

"There's a God dammed herd of cattle coming at us!" he cried out in surprise and alarm.

Jo stood, moving toward the door to see better.

The sky above the southern horizon was gray with dust, and a noise like distant thunder could be heard accompanying the cloud. But the storm that was approaching them wasn't of nature's making. From one edge of the shallow depression to the other, the horizon was filled with the dark brown mass of a thundering herd running in fear and anger directly at them!

DAN HAD TIED a twenty-foot length of heavy rope onto the upright connecting the steel landing skid to the helicopter and had looped it around his body several times before securing it loosely at the other end. He felt secure enough perched in his wobbly position on the skid, but that opinion changed drastically as soon as the helicopter lifted off the ground.

The ranch yard dropped precipitously below his dangling feet, the few men remaining in the yard quickly reduced to the size of scurrying ants as the buildings took on toy-like dimensions. Dan had never been in this position before and had never felt so exposed and vulnerable.

But there was no time to think of his own peril now. All he could think of was Jo. The mere thought of her held captive by those ruthless men gave him the resolve to not think about the height at which he flew. Nothing was as important as Jo.

As the craft began to sweep northward over the rolling landscape, Dan began to seriously wonder about his parachute for the first time. He had bought it from a friend who needed the money—more to be a friend than out of need for a parachute. And, since he didn't personally know how to fold a parachute, Dan hadn't checked it. Now here he was about to risk his life on the belief that it was properly folded and not just jammed into the packet in a jumbled mess. For all he knew, nothing but a wad of silk tangled in shroud lines would plop out when he pulled the rip cord.

It was definitely too late to worry about that as they sped toward their destination, climbing as they went. All too soon it would be time to put his faith to the test.

He double-checked the nunchaku, which was still in place in the utility pocket of his fatigue pants. He kept one hand on it as they flew, just to make sure—after all, it was all he had.

They were well over Pettigrew land now, and Dan could see a moving brown mass to the west, dust rising to blur the outline of the herd. No more than three miles beyond the cattle, he could just make out the dark speck that had to be the line shack. They were nearly too late! If they didn't hurry, the herd would pass before he could chute down!

Agent Grimes was apparently aware of the situation, too, for he turned them sharply, taking a more direct route to the north of the cabin. He sped up, too, nearly tearing Dan's grip free of the strut as the rush of wind grew to a sudden blast that tore over him. They banked into the turn, the ground momentarily slipping away as the helicopter tipped up like a bell and back down again. Then they continued toward the shack, aiming just north of it as planned, though they would clearly be arriving much closer than what Dan had requested. The herd would cover their noise, however, for he would be making his jump only minutes before the cattle reached the cabin.

And then they were there, no more than one thousand feet above the ground, and Dan untied one end of the rope and carefully removed the loops from around his body until the rope was hanging loose and blowing away from the skid.

Grimes slowed and then stopped, holding them still in the air while the herd continued to rush toward the shack on the prairie.

Dan grabbed the handhold next to the edge of the canopy and stood slowly, looking in through the Plexiglas at the man at the controls of his helicopter. He gave the agent a quick thumbs-up and a broad, though not quite sincere, grin then pushed himself backward off the strut toward the earth.

At first it seemed as if he wasn't falling but that the helicopter was drawing away from him. It wasn't until he extended his arms and maneuvered himself over that he was really aware of how fast he was falling. The ground seemed about ready to slap him in the face, and he grasped the rip cord frantically.

He nearly pulled the cord, but calmed himself at the last moment. He had to get lower first, because the cattle were too close for him to be drifting slowly down. He had to get down there fast!

Holding his arms out like wings, he twisted his body to fly closer to the cabin, and he slowly counted to ten. Only then did he pull the rip cord and was rewarded by a satisfying jerk at his back, which pulled him upward so that he was looking down between his tennis shoes at the growing cabin below.

Moments later, he hit the ground and rolled, pulling against the pressure of the chute dragging across the ground. He was out of the harness and running, pulling the nunchaku free, while the sound of the approaching cattle grew around him.

He had to get there first! He simply had to!

And as he ran, he could see a faint wisp of smoke rising from the front of the cabin.

WHEN JO SAW THE HERD, she moved quickly, swinging her bound fists against Zane's back as hard as she could and then kicking at the back of his knee. Unfortunately, he spun on her and caught her next blow in his two hands and pulled her tightly against him.

"Gotcha!" He grinned, turning his hip to protect against any further assault. "You had better be ready to get into that truck, or I'll toss you out for the cattle to play pinball with," he hissed. "You understand me?"

"I'd rather take my chances with the cattle than with you," she snapped.

He only smiled, saying, "Then I'll just have to drag you."

"Come on!" Shorty yelled. "There's a pack of drovers behind the herd."

A new sound suddenly cut through the thundering hooves of the approaching cattle, a sound that rattled the windowpanes and enveloped the cabin in a storm of dust. Then a shadow moved over the doorway as the helicopter passed and banked high into a turn over the herd.

"Dan!" Jo yelled out in relief and joy. "That's it," she shouted over the sound of the helicopter passing low overhead again. "It's all over, Kenny!"

"Like hell it is!"

Ken dragged Jo back toward the table, where he picked up the gun and stuffed it into the waistband of his jeans and then started toward the door. Shorty stepped through ahead of them, eager to reach the vehicle that was their only means of escape.

But, as the burly man emerged into the dust storm outside, he suddenly jerked to one side as though he was a marionette whose string had been plucked abruptly.

He snapped back then, spinning into the cabin with blood streaming out of his shattered nose. He fell like a slab of granite at their feet.

"What the hell was that?" Zane looked toward the door and then down at his fallen comrade. Then he smiled and pulled Jo around in front of him and marched her to the door.

She had no idea what had happened to the other man, but it was too late to wonder when she was propelled through the door with a sudden convulsive shove that sent her staggering out into the tumultuous scene outside.

She fell and rolled, looking desperately around her just in time to see Zane dive out behind her with his gun drawn. Just after he emerged, she saw Dan springing up from beside the door even as Zane raised his revolver.

"He's got a gun!" Jo shouted, struggling to get up.

Dan charged him, spinning something in his right hand that moved too fast to be seen. Zane's gun snapped out of his hand and bounced off the cab of the pickup as blood spattered from a magically broken thumb bone. Dan attacked, kicking at Zane's head.

But Zane was fast enough to avoid the blow aimed at his head, and, despite the pain he must have felt, he grasped Dan's leg and pulled him over.

The two men rolled on the ground a moment, then Dan pulled away, slapping one end of his weapon against Zane's head. The other man went the other way. But, instead of diving for the gun, he tackled Jo, knocking her back against the pickup and then turning to use her as a shield.

"Goodbye, hero," Zane said. He pulled Jo against him by her hair as he grappled to open the door of the truck.

"It's not happening," Dan called out. "You're not getting away."

"I can break her neck, if you want me to," Zane promised. He pulled the driver's door open and stepped up against it.

Dan took a step closer, measuring the distance between them and calculating how far he would have to jump to come within striking distance as he continued spinning the weapon in his hand. "You're cut off, Zane," he said. "Nothing but cattle along that road. And there's an FBI agent flying my helicopter overhead to keep track of where you go."

"He can watch me all the way to Canada for all I care," Zane shouted. "But I'm not turning myself in to the likes of you."

Dan took another step as the thunder of the approaching herd grew around them.

Suddenly, Zane stepped sideways and flipped Jo around into the open door of the truck, shoving her onto her stomach across the seat. Dan attacked, his foot flashing out against the man's cheek, followed by two damaging blows to his abdomen. Zane dropped to his knees and rolled beneath the open pickup door, stalling the attack for a moment as Dan dodged to the side to renew his assault.

That moment was all the desperate man needed, however, because he dived onto the gun lying in the dirt and rolled with it, firing once.

"Dan!" Jo screamed out in terror as she saw him spin into the dirt, rolling toward the back of the pickup. "Oh, God, Dan!"

"Forget him!" Zane yelled. He pushed her into the pickup, sitting on her sprawled legs as he twisted the key in the ignition and threw the pickup into gear.

Dan appeared in the open door, grabbing at Zane's arm and nearly pulling him from the vehicle. But the sudden momentum of the truck pulled him off balance, and he fell as Ken jammed the accelerator down. He lay panting in the dirt watching the truck tear away from the shack and the angry might of the herd bearing down on them.

The cattle were almost upon him when Dan stood and tried to stagger to the door of the shack. The bullet had torn through his right leg, however, and the damaged limb wouldn't support him. He fell, struggling to rise again and avoid being trampled.

Then the thunder of his Cobra obliterated all other sounds, as Agent Grimes brought the craft down directly overhead, hovering no more than two feet over the fallen pilot so that the cattle, frightened by the flying beast, had to part and pass them by.

A moment later, they had gone, driven north toward the fleeing pickup by the shouting men of the Bar T who'd been joined by several of Pettigrew's hands.

Grimes landed the helicopter and opened the canopy as Dan stood. "What now?" he yelled.

"Get out!"

Dan pulled himself painfully into the craft as the other man slipped out the other side of the cockpit. A second later, Dan was airborne, scanning the landscape through the dust for any sign of the pickup truck.

He saw it not far ahead of the herd. But his blood froze as he turned the copter toward it. The truck had overturned. Two figures could be seen struggling beside it as the mass of cattle bore down on them!

As soon as they began moving, Jo had started pummeling her captor with her fists. There wasn't much room to put much force behind her blows, but she did manage to interfere with his driving. He thrust her angrily aside, only to have to contend with her fists again and again.

Zane had shoved her across the seat, and he was still sitting on her legs as he drove, so that his head was pressed awkwardly against the ceiling of the cab, making it all the harder to steer with the woman beating at his face. He never saw the rut that caught the wheel of the truck, and he couldn't slow them fast enough to avoid tipping when that hole deepened. Suddenly, the world flipped over, the two people bouncing within the cab until the truck came to a rest upside down in the dry grass.

Jo immediately snaked her way out the window, standing before Zane was able to get out. She kicked him in the chest as he emerged, and was ready to kick again when he ducked and pulled her foot out from under her.

They rolled downhill and fought, but Jo was no match for the man who finally subdued her with a vengeful laugh. Then they both heard the cattle and turned to face them.

Behind the cattle, gaining fast, was Dan's helicopter. He rushed in overhead and dropped on them, coming lower and lower until Jo spotted the rope hanging from the landing gear and dragging across the ground below the helicopter. So that was his plan!

Jo twisted again, stomping the heel of her boot down on the arch of Zane's foot and bursting away from him when his grip slackened a moment. She ran toward the herd and the hemp rope that hung between her and death. With a desperate lunge, she grabbed the rope with both hands and held on for dear life as the helicopter pulled her up, the toes of her boots brushing the backs of the lead cattle in the herd.

Zane tried to run toward the pickup, but he slipped and fell, scrambling frantically to regain his footing. He was about halfway to the vehicle when the trampling hooves of the angry beasts overtook him, and he disappeared within the dust.

Jo hung on to the rope as Dan carried her back about ten feet above the ground until the herd had passed below them. Then he lowered her carefully until she could step down and stand shakily on her feet again.

While the crew of the Bar T leaped from their horses, Dan put his bird down and got out slowly to limp back to her and gather her into his arms.

"You were right," she shouted, laughing. "Texans are indispensable."

"I knew I'd convince you," he replied. Then he kissed her, holding her to him as though no power on earth could ever break them apart again.

"Oh, Dan, your leg! Here, sit down," she exclaimed as she helped him sit. "We'll have to get something for a tourniquet."

"I've got a knife in my pocket. Cut some of that rope from the chopper."

Jo took the knife and rushed to secure a length of rope, as Agent Harden threw open the door of the ranch pickup he was in, stepping out before it had come to a full stop. "Where is he? Where is Ken Zane?"

Dan and Jo looked toward the herd which had begun to slow without the prompting of the cowboys behind them. Hank was returning on horseback, riding without any haste toward the others.

"Where is he?" the agent repeated to Hank as he stopped his horse and pushed his hat back on his head.

"Out there," he replied laconically. "Seems he had a head-on collision with a stampede."

The agent started to walk toward the body, then stopped and returned. "There'll be some sorting out to do yet," he said. "But I think I can safely say that you are hereby exonerated of all pending charges, Miss Tate. And you," he said sternly to Dan, "that was one hell of a grandstand plan you had there, mister. The whole thing was foolhardy from beginning to end. We're both lucky it worked." Then he broke into a grin and held his hand out. "Good job, son," he said. "Damn good job."

"I agree." Jo kissed Dan's cheek as she finished twisting the rope tight around his upper leg. "But I think we better get our hero into town now. And next time you have to rescue me, Daniel, please remember to wear your shining armor."

"I'll remember, boss," he said, laughing. "But I think I'd rather work on keeping you out of trouble to begin with. It may be a lifetime job, but I think I can manage it."

"You are definitely hired!"

"One more thing," he said. "About that date we had to go dancing tomorrow night? Would you mind if I took a rain check on that?"

"Just as long as you don't make a habit of it," Jo replied, laughing. "I guess I can allow it this one time."

Chapter Eighteen

That year's roundup was a tumultuous affair for everyone involved. For the first time in local memory, the Tate and Pettigrew ranches joined forces to herd each other's cattle. Instead of being an arduous task, with three or four men driving thousands of cattle to the fenced land, the process became a rather easy assignment with a ten-man crew, including one airborne wrangler, seeing after the stragglers.

They rounded up Pettigrew's cattle first, since the new estate accountants demanded an accurate count to include in their inventory. After the stampede, the roundup was more difficult, of course. It took two extra days to collect the cattle and then walk them back over the route they had run in half an hour.

It would be the last roundup of a Pettigrew herd. There was no family with any claim or interest in the land, so it was to be sold at auction, either in whole or in parcels, to the highest bidders.

After the cattle were in and counted, and the prairie dust had settled over the Pettigrew spread, the cowboys moved over to the Bar T to complete the task there, as well.

"Flyboy, this is Jo. Do you read me?"

Jo sat atop Dorothy Parker on a ridge overlooking the vast herd of Bar T cattle grazing along the shallow valley. The lowing of the cattle drifted up to her like the veil of dust that rose above them, a faintly romantic sound carried by the breeze. Behind her, she could hear the faint sound of the people gathered at the traditional Bar T roundup barbecue.

She didn't know how anyone could live a complete life without this; she knew very well that she could not.

"Flyboy," she called again, "are you guys coming down here or not? There's a line forming."

"Here we come, Jo." Dan's voice came back to her on the radio. "One second."

The distant speck of the helicopter began to grow, swelling swiftly as he flew high over the herd and then dived toward her position on the ridge. With a thundering rush of wind, he passed overhead, tilted into a short turn and then hovered before beginning to come slowly to earth again. A moment later, the craft was at rest, its rotor blades slowing to a halt.

"What's up?" Dan opened the canopy and slowly stepped out, hampered by the cast covering most of his right leg. He stood hopping on his good leg and holding the other off the ground. "We were just getting into it."

"I think your boss is a party pooper." Doc Hollander handed Dan's cane down to him and then moved himself out of the helicopter to stand beside the pilot. "That was great, son!" he exclaimed, clapping Dan on the shoulder with a broad grin. "Anytime you need someone riding shotgun, I'm your man."

"Just say the word," Dan replied, laughing. "I'll manage to scare you yet."

"Almost had me on that one dive," the veterinarian admitted. "That first dive was one hell of a ride, but you chickened out too soon."

"Both of you are hopeless," Jo said as she rode up to him. "How anyone could enjoy flying in that contraption is beyond me. It's like riding in a roller coaster."

"Doc's right, you are a party pooper." Dan patted the neck of Jo's mount as she swung her leg over and stepped down beside him. "But a beautiful one." He gathered her into his arms, kissing her deeply, stopping only when the vet cleared his throat.

"I'm an old man," he told them, smiling. "All that smooching isn't good for my blood pressure."

"But helicopter rides are no problem?" Jo said.

"It was like a walk in the park," the older man said.

"You just wait until next time," Dan promised. "When I've got both my legs back, you'll pay for that insult."

"Well, in the meantime, stop leaning on that leg and use the cane," Doc Hollander said. "Bullet wounds aren't laughing matters, you know, young man. Does it pain you much?"

"Not at all," Dan told him, holding Jo to his side tightly. "I'm in top form."

"And you told me he wasn't a cowboy, Jo," the vet said, smiling broadly. "He lies like a cowboy, though, doesn't he?"

"Maybe, but then who wants to listen to a grown man whine about his little aches and pains," she replied. "I suspect he'll speak up if he needs to."

"What about the cattle, Doc?" Dan asked, changing the subject. "Are they cleared yet?"

"We tested one in fifty of the Pettigrew herd and didn't find any residual chemicals," the older man replied thoughtfully. "According to what that fellow, Shorty, told us, all they dumped was shale refinery waste. Any cows that ate some of that would have died, so there wasn't much point in testing at all. Of course, the whole herd has been sprayed to remove any residue on their hooves or legs. I don't think there will be any problem with the FDA."

"And our herd never was in contact," Jo added. "Thank God for that."

"If Zane and his pal would have just buried the cows on the ranch instead of trying to blame it on you, they'd have been all right," Doc Hollander said.

"They only did that to try to shut Pettigrew up," Dan said. "He already knew about the dead cattle, so they had to make it look like it happened on the Bar T so he would quit worrying about his spread."

"I think he felt too guilty about what he was allowing them to do to fall for the cover-up," Jo said. "He was a bothersome man and a bad neighbor, but he was a rancher at heart. He couldn't have gone through with poisoning the land like that."

"No," the veterinarian agreed, "he couldn't have. Well, I'm going to get me some of that barbecue before it's gone. Flying kinda makes me hungry."

"You're going to be a tough customer up there, aren't you?" Dan asked. "But I'll get you yet."

The vet waved happily as he walked toward the people gathered around the grills and tables set up on the prairie just outside the ranch compound. Most of the town had shown up, many of them taking advantage of the carnival atmosphere to get rides in Dan's helicopter. More than a few of them had regretted the decision, much to the pilot's amusement. Now it appeared that it was Hanks' turn, since he and Andrew Hollander were walking toward them as Doc walked away.

"Oh, boy," Dan shouted toward them. "New victims."

"Just one," Hank told him as he walked up to the helicopter. "I don't think Andrew is quite up to it yet."

"No way," the lawman said. He, too, was using a cane to help support his weight as he walked, but he appeared to have recovered well. "I already had my ride."

"Get in, hombre," Dan said to Hank. "You know, I could probably squeeze your lady in with you if you want to take her along. There's nothing quite like a helicopter ride to get a woman's arms around you."

"No, Mary's busy with the barbecue," Hank said. "Besides, she's not afraid of anything. A couple dips in a helicopter won't mean nothing."

As Dan was getting back into his craft, Hank leaned toward Jo and quietly said, "I have to talk to you about something later if you've got time."

"You planning to put a bid in?" she asked him.

"Yes, I thought I might if the bank will back me," he replied. He looked toward the helicopter and then back to her, smiling. "You don't need two foremen on the ranch, anyway."

"You go ahead." Jo put her arms around him, hugging him tightly to her. "And if you need help with the bank, just give a holler."

"Thank you," he said. He stepped back, somewhat embarrassed by her embrace. "Thanks a lot."

"Hey!" Dan shouted. "What are you doing with my woman, you dirty cowpoke!"

"None of your business!" Hank shouted back as he ran over and climbed up to the cockpit. "Now how do I strap myself into this contraption?"

Jo turned away as they pulled the canopy shut and switched the rotor blades into action. She looked at Andrew for a moment, frowning, and then walked to his side and stood watching the craft leave the ground.

"When are you going to tell them?" Jo asked when the noise of the vehicle was gone.

"Tell who what?" Andrew stiffened at her side, looking down at the people eating their meals.

"You know what I mean, Andrew. There's no sense thinking you can get away with it."

The lawman sighed, shaking his head. He glanced toward her but looked away again quickly, unable to meet her gaze.

"I don't know," he said at last. "I haven't quite got up the nerve yet."

"Shorty isn't talking yet," Jo said. "But he's got a good lawyer. Good lawyers make good deals, and the best deal he can get is to start naming names. We both know whose name will come out first."

"It seemed so easy to just look the other way," Andrew said sadly. "Just a couple trucks a month. A thousand dollars each. It seemed like easy money."

"It would have been," Jo agreed. "If you could live with yourself afterward."

"I picked out the site for them," he said. "That's all clay there. It wouldn't get through that."

"Maybe not, but how long would it have been before they had to move to a different site?"

"I was going to cut them off if they did."

"They would have just cut you off like they did Pettigrew."

"At least I would have gone down doing my job then," he said. "Like I almost did."

"I should have guessed what you were up to when you charged in like that," she said. "It wasn't like you to expose yourself unwisely, and it really didn't make sense for Shorty to fire at you unless he thought you had double-crossed him. He should have just run."

"I figured I could either kill him or he'd kill me." Andrew looked at her then, the sunset adding a hue of regret to his tired eyes. "Your boyfriend wasted a flight."

"No, he didn't." Jo put her hand on his shoulder, squeezing his arm. "I'd hate to lose you no matter what you did. Besides, you came around when we needed you."

"How did you figure it out?"

"They had to have someone on the force working for them in order to avoid trouble with the trucks. I thought it was Glen," she said. "I didn't really put it together until later. But, if it wasn't Glen, then you were the only real choice left. The best choice, really."

"Glen was always screwing things up, but in the end he did a better job than I did."

"He was trying to do his duty at the end," Jo said.

"If I had known it would come to murder, I would never have signed on," Andrew said. "And when we turned up your father's shotgun on the range, I damn near chucked it all right then."

"Why didn't you?"

"I had to find a way to get out of it clean. Believe me, Jo, if it had actually come to arresting you for the murder, I would have stopped it."

"I believe you, Andrew. But why did you ever get mixed up in it? You had a position of respect here. Why throw it away?"

"For you," he said quietly.

"Me?"

"I wanted to get something for myself, some kind of a stake. I thought, well, I guess I didn't want to look like I was after your money. I wanted to be able to offer you something more than a sheriff's salary."

"Oh, Andrew, I'm so sorry."

"You've got nothing to be sorry about," he replied. "You made it clear enough the first time I proposed. I just hoped I could change your mind."

"It wasn't that I didn't like you, Andrew," Jo said. "Just that I didn't love you. Money wouldn't have changed that."

"No, and I should have known you better than to think it would. Still, I had my hopes." Then he laughed, shrugging. "When I saw you and Dan together like that, I finally knew I was being a damn fool. I figured I might as well do my job or die trying."

"You did all right at the end," Jo assured him. "You really did."

"It's ironic that you ended up hitching up with a fella with more money than you have," Andrew said.

"What do you mean?"

"Oh, I checked him out as soon as I heard he was coming," he explained. "The Fitzpatrick family spread is over twice the size of what you've got. Oil, too. And then there's Dan's old man. He runs a top-notch brokerage house in Texas."

"I didn't know," she said.

"No, I don't suppose you did. But then, how many pilots have the cash to buy a helicopter like that one? Surplus or not, it's got a hefty price tag."

"Dan doesn't talk much about money," Jo said, smiling.

"No, he wouldn't. He's the type of man who values his own work, and doesn't put much stock in what his relatives might hand down to him. You've got a good man there, Jo. Better than what you would have had in me."

"You're not so bad," she said, watching the black speck of the helicopter turning against the setting sun. "And you can prove that by stepping forward and doing the right thing."

"I will," he said. "I wanted to say goodbye first, is all."

"I'm glad you did," she said. "If you need a character witness, I'm here for you."

"Jo, you're too good to be believed."

"Hey," Jo said then, throwing her hand up to shield her eyes as she stared at the approaching helicopter. "Oh, no, he wouldn't!"

Jo ran, leaving the sheriff standing perplexed on the hill as she hurried, laughing, toward the crowd by the tables. "Hit the dirt!" she cried out.

The helicopter buzzed the tables just as she reached them, rushing overhead no more than ten feet above the ground while the party-goers ducked and dived, the children laughing at the confusion. When the craft turned and stopped, Jo could clearly see the sick expression on Hank's face. Behind him, her man sat, grinning.

Dan gave her a thumbs-up through the window as he brought the craft back to the ground. Grinning, Jo returned the sign.

And as the townspeople stood, knocking the dust from their clothes and smiling at one another, Jo thought it actually was a fairly humorous joke at that.

She also couldn't stop thinking about what a lucky woman she was—she'd finally found the one man who could make her truly happy. As she gazed up at his helicopter, she reflected on his courage, his humor, and his passion—yes, especially his passion—and she knew, without a doubt, that Daniel Fitzpatrick was everything she'd ever need or want. He was her soul mate . . . for life.

HARLEQUIN®

I N T R I G U E®

COMING NEXT MONTH

#281 HUNTER'S MOON by Dawn Stewardson
Timeless Love
Dani Patton awoke to the strangest circumstances: she'd traveled through time to 1850 Transylvania, and hooded villagers—convinced she was a vampire—were about to drive a stake through her heart! Rescued by sexy Count Nicholae, Dani's only hope was to convince him vampires didn't exist...but a live killer did!

#282 DOMINOES by Laura Gordon
There was nothing P.I. Kelsey St. James enjoyed more than solving a case. Except when her best friend was the victim. Ben Tanner, a Chicago cop with an attitude, had his hands full with Kelsey, for if he was right, *she* would be the next to topple....

#283 SILENT SEA by Patricia Rosemoor
Dolphin trainer Marissa Gilmore was at home in the sea—until someone tried to kill her. Was it only coincidence that Riley O'Hare was near every attempt on her life...or did the sexy owner of Dolphin Haven have secrets of his own?

#284 LOOKS ARE DECEIVING by Maggie Ferguson
A Woman of Mystery
Alissa Adams was afraid to sleep. In her nightmares she saw the face of the next day's murder victim. Kyle Stone wanted to believe her—and to love her—but a detective needed hard evidence. And then Alissa's own face appeared in her dreams....

AVAILABLE THIS MONTH:

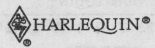

HARLEQUIN®

I N T R I G U E®

*When lovers are fated, not even
time can separate them....When
a mystery is pending, only time
can solve it....*

Timeless Love

Harlequin Intrigue is proud to
bring you this exciting new program
of time-travel romantic mysteries!

Be on time in July for the next book
in this series:

**#281 HUNTER'S MOON
by Dawn Stewardson**

Better take a garlic necklace along
when you travel back to drafty dark
castles in remote Transylvania. You
never know if you'll come face-to-
face with a thirsty vampire!

Watch for
HUNTER'S MOON...
and all the upcoming books in
TIMELESS LOVE.

TLOVE3R

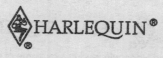

HARLEQUIN®

Weddings, Inc.

EXPECTATIONS
Shannon Waverly

Eternity, Massachusetts, is a town with something
special going for it. According to legend, those who
marry in Eternity's chapel are destined for a lifetime of
happiness. As long as the legend holds true, couples
will continue to flock here to marry and local
businesses will thrive.

Unfortunately for the town, Marion and Geoffrey Kent
are about to prove the legend wrong!

EXPECTATIONS, available in July from
Harlequin Romance®, is the second book in
Harlequin's new cross-line series, **WEDDINGS, INC.**
Be sure to look for the third book, **WEDDING
SONG,** by
Vicki Lewis Thompson (Harlequin Temptation® #502),
coming in August.

WED-2

HARLEQUIN®

Don't miss these Harlequin favorites by some of our most
distinguished authors!
And now, you can receive a discount by ordering two or more titles!

HT #25551	THE OTHER WOMAN by Candace Schuler	$2.99	☐
HT #25539	FOOLS RUSH IN by Vicki Lewis Thompson	$2.99	☐
HP #11550	THE GOLDEN GREEK by Sally Wentworth	$2.89	☐
HP #11603	PAST ALL REASON by Kay Thorpe	$2.99	☐
HR #03228	MEANT FOR EACH OTHER by Rebecca Winters	$2.89	☐
HR #03268	THE BAD PENNY by Susan Fox	$2.99	☐
HS #70532	TOUCH THE DAWN by Karen Young	$3.39	
HS #70540	FOR THE LOVE OF IVY by Barbara Kaye	$3.39	
HI #22177	MINDGAME by Laura Pender	$2.79	
HI #22214	TO DIE FOR by M.J. Rodgers	$2.89	
HAR #16421	HAPPY NEW YEAR, DARLING by Margaret St. George	$3.29	☐
HAR #16507	THE UNEXPECTED GROOM by Muriel Jensen	$3.50	☐
HH #28774	SPINDRIFT by Miranda Jarrett	$3.99	☐
HH #28782	SWEET SENSATIONS by Julie Tetel	$3.99	☐

Harlequin Promotional Titles

#83259	UNTAMED MAVERICK HEARTS (Short-story collection featuring Heather Graham Pozzessere, Patricia Potter, Joan Johnston)	$4.99	☐

(limited quantities available on certain titles)

	AMOUNT	$
DEDUCT:	10% DISCOUNT FOR 2+ BOOKS	$
	POSTAGE & HANDLING	$
	($1.00 for one book, 50¢ for each additional)	
	APPLICABLE TAXES*	$ _____
	TOTAL PAYABLE	$ _____
	(check or money order—please do not send cash)	

To order, complete this form and send it, along with a check or money order for the
total above, payable to Harlequin Books, to: **In the U.S.:** 3010 Walden Avenue,
P.O. Box 9047, Buffalo, NY 14269-9047; **In Canada:** P.O. Box 613, Fort Erie, Ontario,
L2A 5X3.

Name: _____

Address: _____ City: _____

State/Prov.: _____ Zip/Postal Code: _____

*New York residents remit applicable sales taxes.
 Canadian residents remit applicable GST and provincial taxes.

HBACK-AJ